DANIELLE BROOKS

Smoke Signals
A Lovey's Bay Romance

First published by Danielle Brooks Writes 2024

Copyright © 2024 by Danielle Brooks

All rights reserved. No part of this publication may be reproduced, stored or transmitted in any form or by any means, electronic, mechanical, photocopying, recording, scanning, or otherwise without written permission from the publisher. It is illegal to copy this book, post it to a website, or distribute it by any other means without permission.

This novel is entirely a work of fiction. The names, characters and incidents portrayed in it are the work of the author's imagination. Any resemblance to actual persons, living or dead, events or localities is entirely coincidental.

Danielle Brooks asserts the moral right to be identified as the author of this work.

First edition

ISBN: 9798333752697

This book was professionally typeset on Reedsy.
Find out more at reedsy.com

"At the heart of experience, there is a fire that burns all we know. Offer everything to that fire, what remains the ashes of love – is that for which we have longed all over life."
— Rupert Spira

"This is now. Now is, all there is. Don't wait for then, strike the spark light the fire."
— Rumi

This book is dedicated to those who feel lost in the haze of love. May your destined partner beam through and find you.

Acknowledgments

Whew! This release had a surreal feeling around it as it marks my 5th release in the year 2024. To look back and realize I published my first book in February and now on my 5th, it's so so surreal to me, but here we are!

Thank you to my sister, Demetra. She hears my ideas before anyone else and listens and encourages me every time. I appreciate your love and support more than you know.

Thank you to my children. They also listen to my rambles about my books, particularly my son Sage, who's old enough to understand the concepts. I thank them for believing in Mommy and expressing how proud they are of me.

Last but certainly not least, all my book friends. Not fans, but friends because you all mean so much more to me than that. Thank you for rocking with me and loving on my work each and every time. You give the extra boost when my days are chaotic, when my motivation is low, to keep moving and creating. I love you all deep!

Now, enjoy Nina + Denzel

One

Nina

"Can you get a refund?"

"I'm not getting a refund. It was only one night," I argued with my neighbor and good friend, Joni, still busying myself with my task at hand. I momentarily moved my eyes up to her, squinting my disapproval of her question. She leaned against my kitchen's center island counter, returning a look. Hers was paired with a freshly arched eyebrow reaching for the sky, reiterating her question.

"Tuh," she scoffed, her voice dripping with sarcasm. "One night of almost losing your apartment trying to do something you have no business doing."

My eyes rounded as I exclaimed, "Cooking?!"

"Some things just ain't your ministry," she proclaimed matter-of-factly before bouncing her shoulders with laughter. Her amusement was infectious, causing me to relinquish my scowl for a chuckle.

She was right. Cooking was not quite my expertise. It was an heirloom that my mother passed down to me: the gift of having no cooking skills. I recently decided to do something about that by signing

Smoke Signals

up for Chef Monie B. of *Monie B. Cookin'* 4-week virtual cooking class. Chef Monie was one of my favorite chefs to follow via Instagram, but she was far from a kitchen influencer. She was a Michelin-star chef who had traveled the world, tasting and learning several international flavors. Of course, I could learn to cook from one of the top chefs through a series of virtual classes. This is what I told myself, but the way my kitchen almost turned into a smokehouse during the first class, perhaps I was overzealous.

I looked up at the remnants of dark soot, an eye-sore reminder of last week's debacle staining the ceiling above my stove. I really needed to put a little more elbow grease into trying to remove more of the stain before calling maintenance to paint over it. Not only did it ruin my aesthetics, but it also shattered my already deflating confidence. Joni's doubtful eyes on me did not help either.

I poked my lip out, falling into my feelings.

"Joni, don't do me like that. It's my Moment of Yes, remember?"

Her voice was laced with skepticism when she asked, "There's nothing else you can say yes to, Miss Fire Is My First Name?"

My mouth opened, but there was no rebuttal because her joke was actually factual. My mother named me Nina because she learned it was the name of a goddess of fire. Hell, maybe this isn't a heirloom but a jinx that my mom passed down to me with that name. Deciding against finding a comeback, I walked around the counter and to my refrigerator, grabbing the ingredients for tonight's class.

"Are you going to help me with class or stand around and talk about my non-existent cooking skills all night?"

"Aww, Nini, you know I'm playing with you," Joni cooed, wrapping her arm around my shoulder and squeezing me before she managed to drop one last joke on me. "The fire department *did say* you need some supervision next time you're in the kitchen."

I narrowed my eyes at her and nudged her in her rib cage. She doubles

2

over and cackles at her own joke. Unamused, I let out a dry, sarcastic laugh.

"Ha. Ha. That's not even funny, and it wasn't cool for that bubblehead fireman to say that either."

Joni howled as she remembered the comment the fireman made last week as he walked out of my apartment. It wasn't my intention, nor did I think broccolini could burst into a high flame. I remember the man looking at me just as dumbfounded as I felt after he realized it was a vegetable that caused the combustion.

"Maybe next time you should have someone supervise your cooking," I remember him muttering as he walked out of my apartment.

My mouth dropped, and he tried to soften the blow by looking over his shoulder with a smile. When his large frame moved from my apartment door, Joni stood at her front door across the hall, cheeks puffed and holding the laugh she wanted to howl.

Joni slapped the counter, blowing out a breath to calm her current round of laughter.

"Okay, okay. I'm done, and I'm sorry for real."

"Mm-hmm," I hummed, paying her apology no mind, and continued to prepare my prep area. I pulled out my wooden cutting board, a couple of chef knives for preparing the protein and vegetables, and bowls.

"Nina," she sang with an apologetic undertone. "All jokes aside, I'm glad you are doing your "Moment of Yes." Stepping out of your comfort zone..and that funk Pierre had you in."

I cut my eye at her and sneered at the sound of my ex's name.

"This has nothing to do with him but everything to do with me. It's called self-care and self-discovery. Letting the Universe guide me to true happiness by saying yes to new things."

"Yeah, yeah, whatever you want to call it. I'm just glad that Pi—.."

I slanted my eyes tighter at her. She rolled her eyes and waved her hand at me.

"The one formally known as 'That Man' and his funky little engagement is not on your mind anymore."

He wasn't on my mind until Joni brought him up again, but I didn't acknowledge it. Instead, I continued with positivity.

"In the name of saying 'Yes' to all good things, I'm saying 'No' to this conversation about the one who shall stay nameless," I announced, tipping my head up. "Now, can you do something productive? Wash those carrots for me."

Taking my queue to move on from the topic, Joni shrugged her shoulders and took the carrots to the sink to wash. I allowed the sound of the running water to wash away the lingering thoughts of Pierre and refocused on setting up my cooking area. I did not need thoughts of him invading my mind; it's hard enough to cook with my desolate cooking knowledge.

I wandered around the kitchen, grabbed seasonings and paper towels, and then went to my living room to grab my tablet, which I propped up in the center of the kitchen island. I clicked the link to the live stream just in time for Chef Monie to start her introduction. Joni perched herself beside me, leaning on the counter with her head propped onto her hand, while I strained my eyes at the screen as if my eyes would help me hear the chef's instructions better. I inhaled a shaky breath, hoping that this week would be much better than last week.

Tonight's class featured Mediterranean-style pan-seared salmon with roasted potatoes and vegetables of our choice. While I followed Chef Monie's instructions on seasoning the salmon, I had Joni cut the Brussels sprouts in halves and the potatoes in quarters. Feeling good about my seasoned salmon, I grabbed the carrots to chop up while I listened to Chef Monie describe the flavors and what we would do next.

"Look at you," Joni praised as she watched me chop the carrots into bite-size. "You might be aight tonight!"

I smirk at her and laugh through my nose.

"Shush, I need to concentrate."

"Oop, you're right." Joni sings, pretending to zip her lips.

Everything was going great. We finished chopping our vegetables and potatoes, and I combined them into a bowl so Joni could toss them in olive oil and Italian seasoning. Filled with confidence, I listened to Chef Monie instruct us on getting the pan hot enough to sear our salmon. I realized I had not taken my pan out as I turned on the gas stove and wiped my hands with a hand towel. My heart raced at my forgetfulness, and I tossed the towel to hurry over to the undercabinet that contained the pan I wanted to use.

"Shit! Nina...the towel!"

At the sound of Joni's voice, I whipped my head over my shoulder and saw the hand towel in a rapidly growing orange flame over the lit stove burner. My mind had me rushing towards the sink to fill anything with water to diminish the fire, but my body had not caught up with my mind. Instead, I stood frozen, watching the fire whip higher and spread.

"Nini! What the hell are you doing?"

Joni pushes past me as the piercing shrill of my fire alarm goes off and breaks me from my trance. This is when my mind caught up to the reality of the fire and smoke billowing. Joni pushes past me, trying to get the overflowing bowl of water in her hands to the fire. Being hit with an adrenaline rush, I grab the nearest bottle, rush in front of Joni, and toss the contents.

"That's oil, Nina!"

It was too late. The stove lit up like a hibachi dinner show.

Two

Denzel

"Shiiit, ain't no way Drake coming back after "Not Like Us.""
"But he did! You ain't hear the new jawn he dropped?"
"I did…and it was garbage!"

The open space kitchen filled with the echo of roaring laughter as Farris and Deacon continued debating the recent rap battle.

"What were *you* listening to?" Farris spat out, pointing his chopsticks at Deacon.

Deacon's eyes ballooned as he leaned back onto the island counter. "Nigga, what were youuu listening to? Go clean the crusty wax out of your ears because you got to be hard of hearing if you thought that was anything close to Kendrick's joint!"

The crew cracked up again at Deacon's roast of Farris. Farris's eyes narrowed, showing his slight annoyance at him being the butt of the joke.

He shot back, "Yeah, well, you need some soap for that mouth, Mr. Holier Than Thou. What happened to your religion with all that shit talkin'."

A couple of "Ooos" rolled through the crew, egging on the banter. Deacon stabbed his fork into his takeout box of orange chicken and popped the chicken into his mouth. He chewed with his smirk still planted on his face and eyes on Farris as if observing how he had bent Farris out of shape.

"The Lord knows my heart, and He knows I'm still a work in progress." He paused for dramatic purposes and then said, "With that being said, keep your crusty ear wax because I'm naming you Crusty the Clown for your wack ass joke and your wack ass taste of music!"

"Oooh!"

The room sounds off again, and I sit back and chuckle while I watch a scene that happens at least once a week. Captain Benjamin Deacon was always at someone's neck, mostly the rookies. Fireman Landon Farris was the victim tonight, as he has on many occasions, as their banter about music singled him out. I personally think Deacon meant any malice, only to somewhat haze Farris, considering he is the youngest and newest of our crew. Usually, Farris doesn't take it to heart, but tonight, after he threw a shot at Deacon's spiritual life, I could tell he was in his feelings a little.

Deacon was legit the deacon of our crew, being the first to pray over a crew before we started our day. However, he didn't hold any banter or smack talk for anyone, so Farris's dig barely scratched the surface of Deacon's tough skin. Deacon continued to munch on his takeout with his ego on full display.

He waved off Deacon's comeback, causing the banter and spotlight to die from around Farris. He sulked in my direction, his head hanging slightly in defeat. He swung his empty takeout box as he walked to what I knew was a trash can behind me. I stood up and caught him by the arm before he passed me.

"Yo, Farris, don't let it get to you. You know Deac is just fuckin' with you."

"Yeah, I know. Ain't nobody worried about Deac," Farris grumbles, nodding slowly.

I let him continue his path while I went over to the sink to clean out the meal prep container I had just wiped clean of the chicken, jasmine rice, and broccoli. Deacon was standing alongside the counter by the sink now on another topic of conversation.

"Shit, I'm glad I'm settled with my Nessa. Ol' girl is bad, but how you know it's her?"

He passes the phone that belonged to another regular culprit of his, Tevin. From my glance, it was lit up with a picture of a woman with long hair in a red dress that hugged her voluptuous curves. It appeared that he was on the dating app Buzz.

Tevin sucked his teeth. "Man, it is her. You see the check mark? That means she's verified."

After shaking some of the water off the container and top, I placed it in the sink and then turned and leaned against the counter to join in on the conversation quietly.

"Yeah, aight. Good luck with it, though, young blood." Deacon lifted his head and screwed his mouth up as he looked at Tevin with disbelief before he cracked a smile, showing the humor behind his remarks. Noticing me standing beside him, he turned his attention to me with a nudge. "You on that Buzz app, Denzel?"

A laugh skirts out of my mouth, partially because I was taken aback by being included in the conversation. I had no plans actually to partake but only to listen, but here I was.

"Nah, man. I'm coolin' right now."

"Coolin'? It's June, and sundress season has begun. Defrost, my guy!" Tevin chimed in, raising his eyebrows to emphasize his bewilderment at my response.

"Little Tevin has a point," Deacon agreed while at the same time joking about our 5'6 mate. Tevin's mouth dropped as Deacon continued. "It's been, what? Four months since Thandie has been gone? Unless you're still straddling the fence..."

"Nah, that's done," I quickly answer, shaking my head. We were done, although the thought of Thandie still not returning the key to the house or picking up the last of her boxes made it feel like the door wasn't completely closed.

"Bruh, then you need to get on Buzz," Tevin said, patting me on the shoulder while walking off, leaving me as Deacon's next victim.

Deacon crossed his arms and legs while he zeroed in on me. "Be real with me. You still fuckin' around with Thandie, aren't you?"

I scoffed and deadpanned on him. "Nah, man. That's done, like I said. *Done done.*"

Deacon narrowed his eyes as if looking for the lie, but it was the truth...this time. I understood Deac's doubt about Thandie and my relationship. For a year and a half, we played this cat-and-mouse chasing game. I was the cat, trying to get a hold of Thandie. I wanted to settle down and start a family. Hell, I even bought a home in Lovey Bay's new beachside community for us. We were on...we were off. Eventually, I got tired of the chase and Thandie's run-around answers to my desire to get married. She even hit me with the "It's not you...it's me", further twisting the knife into my heart and solidifying my stance on the good guys finish last.

Deacon's pensive look let up when he realized I wasn't lying.

"So, get back out there. Don't let Thandie's indecisive ass keep you from living life."

"I hear you, Deac," I said passively, hoping to move on from talking about Thandie and my lack of a dating life. It wasn't that I didn't want to date. Deac hit part of the reason for my slow move to get back out there on the nose: Thandie and her rejection. I hate being rejected, especially after I become vulnerable and show my heart. Thandie's games with my heart and her rejection did a small number on me. So,

I've been laying low, not thinking about adding another woman in the mix just yet.

A tone shrilled throughout the station, and red lights illuminated the space, indicating a fire emergency was taking place. Like a light switch, my mind turned off from the conversation and on to taking action as my body habitually zoomed past the other crew members towards the corner where my turnout gear was hanging. We were all in the fire engines heading to our destination in less than five minutes.

"Damn! That's the same apartment we were at last week!" Tevin yelled over the siren as he looked at the GPS.

Deacon glanced at the screen and belted out a laugh.

"Ha! Sure is."

"Honey's cute, but she needs to hang up her apron," Tevin quipped with an animated laugh. He was laughing so hard he was holding his stomach.

"What? What did I miss?" I asked, laughing off the strength that Tevin was still dying and Deacon's shoulders were bouncing. I had no idea who "Honey" was or their clear history with her, considering I was off last week.

Deacon rounded the corner. "Oh yeah, you weren't on the shift with us last week. We got a call from this same address for a pretty butter pecan thing…, and I mean, she's pretty! But she can't cook worth a lick! She nearly burnt her kitchen down over some fancy broccoli."

The truck broke out into laughter.

"Damn," I said, feeling bad for the woman. We get a lot of calls, and for them to remember her is…a little embarrassing.

"Yeah, let's see what we got going on tonight," Deacon says after huffing his last laugh and parking the truck in front of Bayside Apartments. I peered through the window at the luxury apartment complex, seeing no signs of flames, but we hustled out of the truck with urgency.

Entering the apartment building, we traveled up to the second floor, still finding no signs of distress. Once we were in front of apartment 215, it still seemed as though things were fairly decent. However, the stench of something burning could be smelled. I took the lead and knocked firmly on the door.

"Fire Department!" I announced after rapping my knuckles on the door. It was only a few seconds before the door swung open, and I was met with the almond-shaped eyes of a beauty. Her face showed shock and embarrassment as her eyes widened and then faltered to her feet as she nervously ran her fingers through her tapered dark curls.

"I-I'm sorry to have you guys come out here again. This is so embarrassing," she stammered.

I could hear Tevin snickering behind me, and I could tell she did, too, by how she tried to cover her face with her free hand while still holding the door knob with the other, blocking the entryway.

I caught secondhand embarrassment for her thinking about what the guys told me on the way here, and I'm sure it was heard in my voice.

"It's okay, ma'am. Can we come in to make sure everything is okay?"

I towered over her petite frame by probably five inches, so the route of her eyes up my body seemed slow-motion, but when our eyes met, the zap of attraction was instant. Her cinnamon-shaded eyes were spell-binding, twinkling with a glint of gold. It contrasted uniquely yet beautifully against her skin. As Deacon described, her skin tone was like butter pecan, and it looked smooth and supple, like soft leather. Her face glowed, perhaps from the heat of the fire...

The fire, Denzel. The fire.

"May I?" I asked once more, mostly for myself and to return my thoughts to my job.

She pushed out a short breath, which caused my eye to twitch in wonder if she had been trapped in whatever haze had come between us.

"Yes, of course. Come in."

She put her hand on her forehead and quickly waved for me to come in before stepping aside. As Tevin, Deacon, and I stepped into the hazy apartment, I noticed her flustered appearance, which caused me some concern.

"Do you mind if I check your vitals while my partners take a look at your kitchen? "

Three

Nina

Shit. He thinks something's wrong with me. The only thing wrong is that his fine ass has me hot and bothered.

I was hoping that the heart palpitations beating my chest up would be the only sign of how this amazon of a man was warming my insides, but then, I did get physically hot.

"Uh, sure," I clamored over my words, sure to add to the idea that my vitals needed to be checked. I huffed my frustration with myself and quickly tried to recover. "I'm really fine, though."

"You are," he said in an almost murmur with a slight curve to his mouth. His dark, auburn eyes met mine again with a twinkle that glimmered brighter than the perfect set of teeth he displayed between his lips. He clears his throat with a short, throaty laugh. "But just to be safe…"

"..Yeah…safe…"

The words slid off of my tongue by way of a swoon-filled breath, and then I silently scoffed at myself as I realized how off-kilt I was over this man. He didn't allow me much time to center my swoon as he gently

Smoke Signals

took me by the elbow and guided me to the nearby dining room table, helping me into a chair. He squatted down in front of me as his big hands wrapped around my wrists to feel for my pulse. He placed a firm yet soft pressure, sending a signal down my body to parts that hadn't been touched for several months. A slow whistle of air seeped through the slither of my parted lips as he looked up at me.

Thank God the vital check required checking the pulse in my wrists and not the pulse in my pussy. Good grief, Nina. Pull it together.

"You seem to be in good shape. Perhaps just a little worked up from the scare, Ms.—"

"Nina," I introduced myself.

"Nina. Fire goddess," he repeated, his voice going up an octave.

I squinted my eyes at him and chuckled in confusion as I questioned, "What?"

"Your name. It's the name of an Incan goddess. Ancient mythology was a favorite subject of mine in school."

He snickered and looked away. His warm brown-hued skin unearthed his red undertone as his cheeks warmed with what I thought was embarrassment. For me, it unearthed a quake in my shoulders over the deep dimple that pierced his cheek, which would've been hidden if he hadn't sported a cleanly shaven face. Between that and his fun fact about my name, I was swooning….and leaking inside. This gorgeous fireman squatting kitty level in front of me with this electrifying smile had the seat of my panties wet.

"Well," I started with a short laugh and a clench of my southern lips. "I guess there was no way around me being a walking fire hazard, eh?"

Behind me, I heard the clunk of heavy boots.

"Ay, Chief. We found the culprit of the fire. This week, it was a hand towel."

"That was her doing. I'm a much better cook, ya know?"

"Oh yeah? You on Buzz?"

Nina

I could hear Joni flirting with the man who announced my clumsy cause of fire at the expense of my lack of cooking skills and squeezed my eyes shut, cursing myself. I would meet a man, a fine fireman, and he finds out I can't cook worth a damn in one visit.

But! This is not about a man. This period in life is about doing things that will make me feel good, and learning how to cook will make me feel good...if I can actually make it without a fire being involved.

The handsome man in front of me hissed through his teeth as he looked over my shoulder toward the kitchen. He looked back at me and said, "This could've been a lot worse, especially with you having a gas stove."

I winced but immediately grew hot as I looked down at his face, which was still at eye level with my love below. She pulsed, and I squeezed my legs further together while sliding out of the chair.

"I know, I know. I just was moving too fast," I rattled off, taking a few steps opposite him while wiping my clammy hands on my jean shorts. I tried to inhale some fresh air to cool myself, but I was hit with the stink of burnt fabric. I was growing more embarrassed by the second of it all. I turned on my heels, now facing Joni, her flirty fireman, and the man causing my inner fire. "I'm sorry I had you all come back out again. This is really, really embarrassing."

I could hear a throated scoff coming from the fireman standing by Joni. With her bulging eyes and twisted lips, she added emphasis on her agreement.

"Tevin," my mythology-spitting hero grumbled. "Round up Deac, and let's head out."

"Here, let me show you to the door," Joni purrs, grabbing hold of the arm of the man I can now identify as Tevin. It is clear she is still flirting, as there is no way to show him out with the open floor plan of my apartment. However, they round up the third fireman and head to the door. I start to follow behind as the nameless fireman trails beside me. Stopping at the door, I turn and note the name on his uniform: Chief Payton.

"I will probably give up my pursuit of cooking after tonight. I want to keep my apartment," I announced, half joking but halfway really considering hanging up my apron.

He flashed his pearly whites before encouraging, "Hey, don't be too hard on yourself. Great chefs are not made overnight but with practice. Just make sure you remember all precautions when you try again."

His smile and the encouragement that glinted in his eyes made me blush and feel less defeated. I bit the side of my mouth before squeaking, "Thanks, uh, Chief Payton."

"Denzel."

I smirked. "Like the actor?"

His silent laugh sneaked through as a bigger smile. He nodded and confirmed, "Yeah, like the actor. My mom loved him so much that she named me after him."

"Damn, I wonder how your Dad felt," I absent-mindedly said. I bit down on my lip after realizing how intrusive of a comment it was, but Denzel belted out a hearty laugh.

"Pops was cool with it," he said once he settled out of his laughter. He stepped across the threshold of my apartment and turned back towards me, still wearing the most gorgeous smile I've seen. "Be safe, Goddess."

I'm sure my cheek's hue deepened as I internally swooned for the hundredth time. If I could change my name to Goddess at that moment, I would, solely on how befitting it felt as it rolled off of his baritone. The tightening of my lips couldn't hide the grin that formed as I thanked him again and watched him amble away just as Joni passed him, strutting back towards me. She glanced over her shoulder after passing Denzel and then turned to me, wearing a devilish grin.

When we were back in the confinement of my apartment, she belted out, "Damn girl, you didn't tell me the fire department was full of *foine*

Nina

men! You holding out on me!"

Joni dramatically fanned herself before leaning onto the island while I tossed my half-prepared food out. I laughed at her, although her sentiments were very true. Lovey's Bay was full of eye-catching black men, but the one who was still on my mind was Chief Denzel Payton.

"Girl, I was too embarrassed to notice the first time."

She added some sass to her voice and asked, "And tonight... you noticed?"

I lifted my eyes from the island countertop I was wiping down and lied. "Barely."

Joni pursed her lips, propping her chin on her hand. "You ain't gotta lie to me, Nina. I saw you and Chocolate Thunder making heart eyes at each other."

I blew a short breath out of my cheeks in an attempt to laugh and scrunched my face with fake confusion. She wasn't falling for it.

"Girl, you aren't fooling anybody. It's okay to look. Hell, it's okay to play. Shit, even I passed that young boy Tevin my number."

My mouth dropped at her revelation. "Girl, what? How do you know he's young?"

"Because he pulled up his Buzz account, wanting me to look for him on it. It said he was twenty-nine. I don't know why he thought I was gonna spend my time swiping through all the profiles to find his. I just made it easy and gave him my number."

"You do like 'em young," I muttered, matter of factly.

"Typically, not this young. I like them to be at least thirty, but hell, he's on the cusp. I'ma live a little." I shook my head at her argument before she turned the focus back on me. "What about Mr. Chocolate?"

"What about him? This era of my life is called Moment of Yes, and the answer to if anything was pursued: No. I damn near burned my apartment down with a hand towel. I am not thinking about a man."

Joni sucked her teeth. "Girl, your summer is gonna be dry just like this heat."

    I threw the wet rag into the sink and leaned against it. I crossed my arms and legs, trying to suppress the thump of my love below as Denzel's face crossed my mind again and fed her an answer that I wasn't too sure I agreed with, "I'm okay with that. "

Four

Denzel

I hated grocery shopping, especially on the weekend. Too many people were in the stores, moseying the aisles and meticulously pondering each item. There was no room for me to bulldoze through to get what I already knew I wanted. And the pick-up option, although convenient, I had no plans to pay a convenience fee for shopping I could complete in less than the hour to two hours it would take to receive the small amount of groceries I shopped for. It was just me, so the grocery list of usually fifteen items didn't make sense to spend more on convenience and tips than it would cost me to shop for them myself.

This is why my typical mid-week grocery store run satisfied my shopping conditions. It usually falls during my 48 hours off my grueling 24-hour work schedule. I'd hit Lovey's Pure Foods Market mid-morning; it was the perfect time as most people are at work, leaving only a handful of delivery shoppers and older people to navigate through. So, when I rolled my cart into the grocery and was greeted by a blast of cool air conditioning, Pharrell singing about being happy, and the sight of almost empty aisles, a content grin crossed my face as I added some pep into my step.

My weekly list was basic and small: vegetables, rice or sweet potatoes, proteins, and a few of my favorite late-night and mid-day snacks. After Thandie and I broke up, she wasn't around to stock up the refrigerator with home-cooked meals or cabinets filled with little snacks and extras that showed someone loved you. I wondered why she did all of that but didn't want to seal the deal with marriage, but she did and didn't. So, when it was all said and done, I stocked my fridge and one cabinet with the necessities I needed. The simple things sufficed when it came to keeping up a mostly healthy habit in my singleness: simple food and workouts.

Although working out was a regular activity in my routine to stay in shape and ready for emergencies, I went a little harder in the gym as a way of therapy after the breakup, you know, to build up some revenge muscles. It wasn't necessarily revenge I was after with cutting up, just a boost to my wounded ego. After all, I had spent a year and a half with someone who practically denied my idea of spending life together. That would hurt any brother who decided to be vulnerable in love. So, instead of fucking every woman I came across in Lovey's Bay, I took my pain out in the gym.

I felt my phone vibrate as I tossed a package of chicken breast into my cart. When I pulled out my phone, fully expecting to see a notification from someone at the station, I frowned, wondering why Thandie was messaging me.

Thandie: Hey, so I was looking for these purple heels. Open-toe sandal. Have you seen them?

Me: No….but I'm sure they could possibly be in one of the boxes you still have here.

Thandie: Oh yeah, I forgot about those. They are probably in there. Lol!

I scoffed inside at her, "forgetting" she still had boxes at the house…and a key. Thandie loved her clothing and shoes; she didn't forget. Part of me feels like this is her way of keeping a pinky toe in so she can tiptoe back in when she's done doing whatever she's doing now. With me not making a big deal over the boxes and the key, maybe a piece of me is still holding on, too.

I slowly rolled my cart while I stared at the screen, trying to decide how or if I would respond. Thinking about it irritated me as it opened up a small cut to allow old feelings to slither in, so I tossed my phone in the phone holder of the shopping cart and got back on my mission of expeditiously getting my shopping done. I rounded the corner to the frozen aisle, nearly colliding with another cart. I grumbled with annoyance but fell short of scowling when my eyes met…

"Goddess."

Nina's eyes rounded with the same surprise she wore the day we met, except now, I'm wondering if it's a surprise or something else. Something else like the wind being knocked out of your body when you encounter something breathtaking, like what's happening to me right now. Those damn hypnotizing eyes. She was effortlessly beautiful in her white tank top, denim shorts, and what seemed to be a bare face.

She bit down on her lip, blushing. "I'm almost sure you forgot my name."

I huffed out a short laugh.

"Never. I'd never forget the name of the goddess of fire, Nina."

Her blush grew into a bashful smile as she looked down at her fidgeting hands. It made her even more gorgeous. She raised her eyes back to mine.

"Good one, Denzel."

I glanced down at her cart. It contained specific herbs, angel hair pasta, shrimp, a bottle of white wine, and a few other things that looked like she was preparing for a date or another cooking adventure.

"Another cooking adventure?" I asked, choosing not to pry with the initial thought.

"Uh, yeah. This week's class is shrimp scampi. Should be easy enough." Her face tensed up with what I thought was her thinking about her past hiccups.

"Yeah, should be," I agreed. "I think you'll have a hard time burning noodles."

I laughed at my joke while she narrowed her eyes at me and dryly said, "Ha, ha. Everyone has jokes."

"Hey, you gotta laugh at yourself sometimes," I said, quieting my laugh. "No, really, it's an easy cook. Just be careful with the wine. Alcohol is flammable."

"Okay, Smokey the Bear," she joked, turning her lip up into a smirk. "I think I can handle a splash of Chardonnay in my sauce."

I chuckled and nodded just as my phone buzzed. I glanced over the screen, seeing Thandie's name light up and another text. I was stuck between looking to see what she sent or continuing to be in the present moment with the gorgeous woman in front of me.

I couldn't lie; running into her again and the light banter we were just engaged in made me want more. It made me want to know her more. It couldn't have been a coincidence that I ran into the woman who had occupied my mind a time or two over the last week. I had wondered a few times if I would run into her again. I thought perhaps if she really were a klutz in the kitchen, I would be called to her apartment again, but running into her here made it easier for me to ask what I did next.

"Well, maybe we can exchange numbers…in case of an emergency…or if you want a little help in the kitchen?"

Five

Nina

"Bittttch! If you don't get those digits!" Joni's overly excited voice shrieks in my ear via my earbuds. "It's your Moment of Yes, remember? Now, say yes!"

I smiled nervously, taking in Denzel's question and Joni's coaching. I was stuck like glue. My heart wanted to say yes, and Denzel's gorgeous face was coercing me to say yes, as was Joni's shrilled voice barking at me to say yes. But my mind was screaming to me, "Hell No!" My mind was trying to keep my head on straight, trying to remind me that my Moment of Yes was about self-care and self-love…but loving yourself means allowing a yes to a brawny man whom I estimated to be standing at about 6'3 tall to my 5'5 stature…right?

"Girl! I know you ain't got that man standing—"

"Sure," I said to Denzel, shutting Joni up.

"Cool," Denzel said, scooping his phone up. He tapped a couple of times and flipped it in my direction so I could type my phone number into an open text thread. He took the phone after I entered it and tapped a few more times with his thumbs. Soon after, I heard a ding from my purse. "I just text you."

* * *

Nina: See you in thirty.

Denzel: You got it.

I placed my phone on the edge of my dresser and stepped back in front of the full-length mirror, scrutinizing my appearance. I wore a cotton sundress that clung loosely over me. It was the literal color of the Tuscan sun and one of my favorite colors to wear, as it illuminated my brown skin to perfection. For some reason, I wanted to look perfect for Denzel.

The idea was still just a thought on Friday night because of my overthinking mind. My mind was still questioning whether this was really part of my plan to indulge in acts of self-love. *Keyword: Self.* That was the phrase that kept popping up in my head every time I thought about it, and then quickly followed up with the point that I spent almost two years with a man who, in the six months after our break up, proposed to another woman. I needed time for self-evaluation.

"Evaluate what? Girl, there is nothing wrong with you," Joni fussed that night when I expressed my indecisiveness.

"I know it's not, but—"

"No buts, Nina. Move on, and I don't mean to be harsh, but then again, I do. When you two first broke up, okay, a little woo-woo here and a woo-woo there, but now, chy, you are getting in your own way."

I winced slightly as I sat mute, staring at my phone. The dead silence on the other end allowed me to sit in what Joni gave me: tough love. That's what Joni always delivered. I don't always want it, but she made a valid point tonight, and I was reluctant to give her the props she deserved.

I had been avoiding eye contact with men, walking past them as if they were non-existent, all because I was psyching myself to believe I wasn't ready. I had more work to do, I told myself. While there were things I could work on, Joni was right. Deep down, I knew nothing was wrong with me. I was a good-ass woman to Pierre. I did all the girlfriend duties, rubbed his back, and washed his God-awful stinky socks. I supported his career endeavors and everything a woman does for a man she wants to be with. I was good to him. It just happened that he was the wrong man to receive that part of me.

So, I told Joni she was right and texted Denzel simultaneously. It was almost like he was sitting with his phone in his hand because he responded right away, and my heart damn near jumped from my chest when his text came through, expressing he was happy that I took up his offer. I didn't know whether to be excited or feel shaded, considering he had first-hand experience seeing how horrible a cook I was. I decided to go with my excited nerves and accept that it was no secret nowadays that I was Chef No-Cook Nina.

I received the text of Denzel's arrival while setting up my tablet on the island counter. Shakily, I typed my response to Denzel, which was a simple thumbs up, and immediately began to question if it was too vague. I didn't understand why I was so nervous; it's not like I've never dated any other men besides Pierre. It's just that I haven't invited a perfect stranger to my home who happens to be a tall, muscular Adonis...

...With a great smile...an Adonis with a great, panty-wetting smile...

I slowly exhaled as I took in Denzel's presence when I opened the door. He had a freshly lined cut, and his hair was swimming in dark, shining waves, and I could've sworn there was a twinkle in his smile. My eyes roamed down his body, taking in the peek of his pectorals through the open buttons of his light blue shirt and then roaming over the curvature of his biceps. My eyes wanted to scan a little lower, but I strayed when I noted the bouquet of assorted flowers and bottle of wine in his hand. I blinked my eyes back to his and warmed up my smile.

Denzel lifted his hands slightly and shrugged his shoulders. "I was told never to show up to someone's home empty-handed."

I creased my lips slightly, appreciative of his sweet gesture, and took the items from his hand.

"Thank you. It's very nice of you. Come in."

Denzel strolled in, and I closed the door behind him. I followed him as he approached the kitchen, surveying the area. My eyes took a gander over his broad shoulders and relaxed-fit jeans until he swiftly turned towards me.

"Place looks a little different without all the smoke," he joked.

I rolled my eyes and sighed through my smile.

"Okay, are we going to do the cooking jokes all night?"

"Nope, last one," he said, chuckling. "Tonight, you will be on your way to being a master chef."

"Ha, that's wishful thinking," I said as I went to the refrigerator.

"It takes one wish to make a way."

I turned to him, scrunched my face into a distorted smile, and asked, "You're full of quotables, aren't you?"

"I like to call them positive affirmations," Denzel corrected, flashing his adorable smile again before I turned back to the refrigerator and opened it, thankful for the blast of cool air.

It wasn't just his physical appearance that kept me flustered. It was the familiarity, the easy banter we shared today, and the few times we chatted before this moment. Our conversation flowed like we had known each other for years, making it very easy for me to be comfortable around him.

Nina

The comfort level was so easy that we moved around the kitchen together like we had done this in our past lives. When the live stream started, we peeled the thawed wild-caught shrimp together as Chef Monie talked through properly cleaning and the importance of deveining the shrimp. Finishing off one of the shrimp, I reached for another in the ice-cold water and found my hand brushing his. The subtle brushing of our skin sent a fleeting shiver through me. Our eyes met and held steady for a beat before we broke the moment with a light chuckle. We both looked down almost simultaneously to find that we had peeled all of the shrimp.

I reached for the empty bowl, but Denzel held up a protesting hand and offered, "I'll clean this up. Do you want to start chopping the onions and garlic?"

I agreed and grabbed the white onion and garlic bulbs. Probably the most gratifying part of my cooking journey is learning how to chop vegetables, so dicing the onions into small squares came to me with ease and pride. However, I was still working on perfecting the garlic. The curve in the herb kept them unsteady under my knife to do anything.

"Here, let me show you a trick."

Denzel's baritone boomed from behind me. Soon after, his sculpted arms appeared one on each side of me. The supple veins in his forearm flexed as he placed a hand on top of mine that held the butt of the knife. The other guided my tiny hand compared to his to the blade's flat. Loosely interlocking his fingers with mine, he added a firm thrust—I mean pressure— crumbling the garlic bulb into smaller pieces. The levee at the seat of my panties crumbled with it.

"Now, you can chop up the garlic," Denzel informed, stepping back and then back beside me, where he gathered the onions into the small prep bowl. I nodded in response as a swooning breath seeped through my lips and began chopping the garlic.

Nina, you are acting like a plumb fool.

I internally chastised myself as I clenched my thighs together, hoping to calm the waves rolling between them. I was glad he could not pick up on the effect he was having on me, but I was still embarrassed as if he could. Granted, it has been a long time since I've been this close to a man, a man that I'm attracted to, to be specific, but it doesn't require me to act like this. It doesn't require every brush of our skin or the simple act of showing me how to level a garlic bulb to prepare to chop to bring on so much.….sexual tension. None of these experiences warranted that, but I'm glad to know that my kitty is still lubricated and not dehydrated after all this time.

The act of cooking went without a hitch. The meal was a simple one: shrimp scampi. Allowing me to lead, Denzel ensured the noodles were cooked to al dente and chaperoned me as I cooked the shrimp. At least, that's how I thought of it, but he didn't treat it that way. Instead of watching over my shoulder, he stood against the counter by the stove, firing off questions.

"So, what do you do?"

Flipping the shrimp one by one in the steaming pan, I answered, "I'm the event coordinator for Lovey's Bay Parks & Recreation."

"Oh, that's dope. So you put together the events like the Farmer's Market?"

I nodded my head. "Yeah, I do, kind of. I approve of the working parts for that event more than anything. Make sure the licenses are in place, and everything goes smoothly." I glanced over at him with a smirk. "I put together the Smokey Blue Bird events for the kids, too."

"Oh, wow, you're behind the Smokey Blue Bird campaign?" He mused with a chuckle. "Pretty cool."

Smokey Blue Bird was the city's fire safety mascot that we used to educate the kids of Lovey's Bay about fire safety. The city coordinated events in conjunction with several fire companies in the town to visit the elementary schools. Considering I have been doing this for a few years, I'm surprised I had never seen Denzel until now.

"Yep," I said, stepping slightly away from the stove yet keeping my eyes on the sizzling pan. Throwing a jab at myself, I said, "Perhaps I need to coordinate an event for adults like me."

Denzel let out a breathy laugh. "Hey, give yourself grace. You're doing pretty good tonight. Look, you didn't even burn the shrimp."

"They are shrimp."

"You'd be surprised how many people mess up shrimp."

We shared a chuckle before the stove timer went off, signaling the pasta was done boiling. I stepped aside to allow Denzel space to grab the stainless steel pot. I watched him carry the steaming pot with two hand towels to the sink and drain the pasta into a strainer, in awe at his comfort in the kitchen. It was attractive to see a man confident and familiar with cooking. Sensing my stare, Denzel looked at me and pierced my heart with another smile. A bashful smirk grows on my face, and I quickly turn to tend to the shrimp that I almost let cook a smidge too long.

We had fallen slightly behind Chef Monie's directions for the meal, but the only thing left was to complete the wine sauce. Remembering her directives, I grabbed the bottle of wine we had uncorked as part of our prep. I was ready to deglaze the pan but stopped abruptly when Denzel's words crossed my mind.

Remember, alcohol is flammable...

"Don't be scared," Denzel softly instructed, walking over to my side. "Pour it slowly into the pan. It will sizzle, but it will die down once it coats the bottom of the pan."

I looked up at him, comforted by his reassurance, and poured it slowly. It did sizzle, causing my heart to quake a little. However, when the fragrant steam wafted to my nose and the sizzle became a simmer, I let go of my restricted breath and smiled. I continued to prepare the sauce by adding a dollop of butter and garlic to the pan and stirring.

"See. Fire Goddess knows how to tame the flame after all."

I bit my bottom lip, trying to tame my smile. In the few times he referred to me as a goddess, I was starting to become smitten by the nickname.

Six

Denzel

I was beginning to wonder if Nina was the Incan goddess reincarnated by how my body temperature fluctuated throughout the night. Yes, we were in the thick of summer, and the June heat was showing out. And yes, we were in a kitchen preparing a warm meal. Neither of those points had anything to do with me mildly perspiring in this well-air-conditioned apartment.

It was the way her cheeks rosed when she was being coy. It was her sense of humor. It was her bold but warm eyes when she looked at me. It was how perfectly rosey-pink her plump bottom lip was, the soft muscle in her arms, and the dip of her chest. And her ass. I tried to be a gentleman, but my gaze fell a few times, noticing how it bubbled under her dress.

Nina was beautiful. I noticed her beauty when we first met, but seeing and experiencing her in her true element was different tonight. It was magnified through everything that she did….and it had me feeling like a simp because I was low-key crushing on her already—typical Denzel. Big, brave firefighter Denzel gets around a beautiful face with a sweet personality and quickly gets wrapped up in the smoky haze of like, of lust…of love.

I never know which one I'm in. I just love the feeling of falling. That has been my demise in love, particularly in my last relationship. I fall, never really knowing if the other party is falling in the same way as me. In my case, I'm falling in hopes of love always. I've always operated with my heart, even when the woman is a baddie. It is bittersweet but true, and from what it seems, relationship after relationship, my quest to fall in love falls short. This is why, as I sit across from Nina on her balcony, sharing the meal we cooked, I am trying to think about everything but what I adore about her—anything to shun away the expansion of my heart.

The sun was nearly at its set now, leaving a shade of fuschia in the sky as the slither of sun disappeared behind Lovey's Bay. The sun setting brought the temperature down a few degrees, and the light breeze made those few degrees feel even lower, making dinner on the balcony comfortable. Nina had a great view of the bay from her apartment, and it was close enough to hear the smooth jazz band holding a concert tonight. Without any effort, it was the perfect ambiance for dinner.

Finishing my plate moments ago, I grabbed my glass of wine and sipped. Nina poked her fork into a lone shrimp, catching a few strings of pasta. She swirled her fork, making a bite-sized mound of her pasta underneath her shrimp, and delicately placed it into her mouth, her lips sliding over the now empty fork. My gaze stayed on her lips, catching the soft sheen the wine sauce created on her lips, and I wondered if her lips were as soft as they appeared. I took a deep breath and pulled my eyes from her lips and onto nothing in particular on the distant beach, trying to forget the thought.

"Mm, I think we did a good job with this," Nina said as I heard her fork clink to the plate.

"I was just the sous chef in your kitchen," I countered. I glanced at her with a half smile that grew into a simper when I caught her dimpled one. *Fuck, I'm a goner.*

"Thanks," she softly replied.

I nodded my head, returning my eyes to the beach. I needed to change the subject so I could look at her without feeling like a teddy bear. "So, are you from Lovey's Bay?"

"Yeah. Born and raised here. What about you?"

"Uh, nah, not really. I am from Stonecrest. It's a small town north of here, about 30 minutes north of Regency—"

"Oh, I've heard of it," Nina said, catching me off guard. I turned to her with raised eyebrows.

"Really? Most of the time, when I mention it, no one has ever heard of it. It's a little country."

"It's a beautiful town. It's been a while since I've been there, but I've been to this farm up there. It has horseback riding and a beautiful lavender field. I can't remember the name of the farm.."

"Henderson Farm," I finished for her, my smile settling a little bigger. "Yeah, that's not far from my family home. So you really know Stonecrest, huh?"

Nina's cute round cheeks lifted again as she nodded quickly, and I chuckled at having someone familiar with my hometown.

"So, how long have you been in The Bay?" Nina asked, leaning forward onto her elbow. Her eyes grew with intrigue, and I fell into them.

"About ten years. I was twenty-two and had just received my bachelor's."

She squinted. "I didn't know you needed a bachelor's to become a firefighter."

"You don't necessarily. I just so happen to have a Bachelor of Science in medicine. It helped me land the job with the company as a firefighter paramedic before becoming Chief."

Smoke Signals

Her eyes grew big as her mouth formed a muted "wow."

"Impressive," she mused.

I lifted one side of my mouth and shrugged modestly. "It's just something I enjoy."

"So you're an ancient mythology and medical student."

I grinned at her, remembering my fun fact from the other day. "Yeah, something like that."

"They don't make them like you anymore. Handsome and smart."

As quickly as her compliment came out, she tried to bite it back by literally biting down on her lip. I smirked and countered with my own.

"I could say the same about you. Beautiful and witty."

Her lips tightened into a smile she tried to conceal as she looked down at her almost empty plate.

"I'm alright," she said.

"*And* humble, too?"

She lifted her eyes to me and rolled them. "Your mom named you right, smooth, just like Denzel."

My laugh bellowed out through the air as she giggled silently. "You're a mess. My name will never let me live."

"No, it's your charm."

Her eyes softened flirtatiously, inviting mine to narrow.

"Well, if it's my charm, then you have to accept that your aura illuminates everything beautiful about you."

We stared holes into each other for a beat before she blinked away and down to her plate again, releasing a soft chuckle and saying, "Perhaps we should clean up the rest of the dishes."

"Sounds like a good idea," I agreed, totally needing a change of pace before I said something else simp-like to this woman.

I followed her into the apartment and the kitchen. We only had a few dishes left out that we hadn't loaded into the dishwasher: our plates and a cooking pan in which we combined the shrimp scampi. She pulled out a meal prep container and gave it to me to pack the leftovers. She filled the sink with more soap than water bath and began cleansing the plates.

"I'll put the leftovers in the fridge for you—"

"No, you take it. Consider it a thank you," I heard her say over my shoulder.

I furrowed my brows, ready to contest the idea, as I turned towards her and protested, "No, I can't do that."

"Yes, you can. I won't take no for an answer."

She turned to me, lifting an eyebrow and pursing her lips. My eyes went to the cluster of soap bubbles nestled between her cheek and the corner of her mouth. I huffed a short laugh as I moved towards her, grinning at how cute and oblivious to this she was. Her eyes rose to meet mine as I stopped in front of her.

Her eyes slightly narrowed with confusion as she asked, "What?"

Without saying anything, I took my thumb and slowly dragged it across the bubbles, taking in how soft her skin was underneath my touch. Her lips parted slightly, our eyes never ceasing to fall short of each other until I moved my gaze to her lips. She took in her bottom lip, letting her teeth graze it as she released it, leaving a glisten from her saliva. I wanted to kiss her, and it seemed as if she wanted to kiss me too by the way her head slightly tilted up and how she didn't move as I gently cupped the side of her face as we grew closer…

…And then the blaring horn of a firetruck siren startled us from the inevitable collision.

We both took a step away from each other. I let my hand drop from her face and then turned to grab the leftovers I no longer wanted to protest about. The siren was my cue to take my ass home before I was putty in her hands.

Seven

Nina

I woke up with my heart racing and my body tingling. I panted as the dream I was abruptly pulled from dissipated particle by particle from my memory. The only thing I could remember was the filthy act Denzel was doing to me, and I was almost…there.

"Grrr!" I growled, rolling my eyes up to my slow, rotating ceiling fan. I banged my fists at my side onto my mattress, frustrated that I couldn't even get past my arousal stimulated by Denzel in my dreams.

I was beyond hot and bothered. I was in heat and needed to cool off from this thing Denzel had caused to take over me. The crazy part is that he did absolutely nothing but be tall, handsome, interesting, muscular…

I clasped my palms over my eyes, hoping I could smack the intrusive picture of Denzel from my head. At this point, I was ashamed of myself for feeling like a fiend for this man. I was fiending for him, hell, just the touch of a man after my dream. The dream was so vivid and felt so real. Even in the waking world, Pierre could never make me feel the way Denzel had me feeling in my sleep state.

Just that thought alone had me wondering what I had been missing during my time with Pierre. Take away the dream, but placing thought on the night before, Denzel was a different type of man than the one I had spent three years with. First, he cooked. Do you realize what a dream it was for a klutz in the kitchen like me? While I do want to be a better cook, the fact that Denzel could cook and was willing to help me learn was a major turn-on. Layer on the fact that he was smart and a hero in his own right. Learning that he was the chief of the local fire company and had a background in medicine said so much about how he had the potential to save a life.

I wish he could save me...

The thought ran through my head as a fleeting memory of my dream crossed my mind. He was saving me in the dream, from what, I don't know, but he had whisked me away from danger. Amid our adrenaline rush, I began to thank him with kisses that led him to receive my gratitude and return it with filthy, unadulterated pleasures.

I exhaled, and another memory from my dream scrolled across my mind, this time centering on the vision of him peeling off my yellow dress as he trailed kisses down my neck and my shoulders and then cupping my breast as he worked circles around my areola. I could remember him looking up at me with fire in his brown eyes as he took my breast in his mouth, pulling his way down to my nipple, where he grazed his teeth against the pebbled point. It made no sense how vivid and real the fading memory was and how quickly it was replaced with another. I fluttered my eyes closed as I parted my legs and succumbed to the journey of my hand to my love below.

This image was of Denzel hoisting me up and my legs around his bare waist just as his thickness entered me. I inhaled a shaky breath as I could imagine myself adjusting to fit him. It was a snug fit but felt so good as he slowly pumped into me, with each pump diving further. And when he had reached my depth, he pumped harder and faster, eliciting whimpers that turned to moans, creating small ways that finally turned into a crashing….

"Oooh…!"

My very real moan pulled me out of my fantasy just as my orgasm sent waves through my body. I fluttered my eyes back to the ceiling fan just as the waves tumbled away, leaving me in a smoky haze of "what the hell" and "goddamn," unsure of what I should even be thinking at this moment. The only thing I could settle on that seemed valid was there was a fire lit for a man I barely knew, and deep down, I was curious if it was burning on his end, too.

Eight

Denzel

"You got it, boss! One more!"

The loud pop of Deacon's hands colliding and his booming "Woo!" was all the ammunition I needed to push 275 pounds of weights from my chest. Deacon assisted on the final ascend, grabbing the weight and placing it back on the rack above my head. I grunted as I pulled myself up to sit, heaving tired breaths.

"Boss, you tired? You're not tired!" Deacon edged on with a taunting smirk. He stood before me now, his arms crossed over his poked-out chest.

"The hell I'm not," I said, through another breath. "I'm spent."

Deacon barked a laugh before slapping me on the back. "Aww, shit. I'm just fuckin' with you. I'd be done after that 275, too. Especially after my midnight press of my ol' lady."

Deacon belted out another laugh, and I joined him. I shook my head at the hint of what his night was like, and all I could say was, "You a wild boy, Deac."

He sits down on the bench behind him. "Hey, what I tell ya'll, boys? I may be a man of God, but a demon still lives in my loins."

Deacon slaps his leg, cracking himself up over his own joke. I couldn't help but chuckle at him. Deacon was one of the most honest and raw brothers I know. You never know what will come out of his mouth, but what you do know is that it isn't a lie.

"I'm surprised you still had the energy for all that last night. I heard shit was crazy this weekend." I said. I grabbed my gallon jug of water and took a swig of the cool water, feeling refreshed from the gulp. He sucked his teeth and proclaimed the opposite.

"Last night was slight work. You know it had to be the rookie's talking about it was crazy."

I shrugged and nodded at the truth of his statement. The weekends can seem a bit wild to the rookies, but to us, we've been doing this for a while. The mishaps of the intoxicated, which was what the crew dealt with mostly this weekend, were the norm and usually aren't life-threatening, just hectic.

"So, whatcha get into this weekend, D?" Deacon asked, moving on.

"I actually had a date this weekend," I admitted, chuckling as my time with Nina replayed. The image of her beautiful face enticed a smirk to heat my face. Before I could straighten out my smirk, Deacon caught it. His eyebrows reached the wrinkle in his forehead.

"My boy went on a date? Okay, tell me who got a nigga smirking and shit."

I dropped and shook my head at Deacon geeking out over my news. I looked up and didn't waste any time giving him the details.

"Her name is Nina. You've met her."

His eyebrows went from high to low as he scrunched them.

"Nina. She's the woman from that apartment—"

Deacon's eyes grew big as he exclaimed, "That pretty thang that can't cook a lick?!"

"She's not that bad, man," I defended, but I still chuckled at his remark.

Denzel

"The date was actually at her house. I helped her cook."

"Good decision," Deacon said with a nod after squeezing some water from his water bottle into his mouth. He continued with his interrogation. "So, how'd this happen? I peeped ya'll giving each other eyes and shit while we were *on the job,* but I didn't think you'd actually try to get her number."

"I didn't. Ironically, I ran into her while I was at the grocery store. I got her number then."

He nodded intently as I gave him a few details about the date, leaving out the part where we almost shared a kiss. I wish I had gone for the kill and kissed her, sirens blaring and all. I burned for the opportunity to feel her lips against mine that night, even well after I left.

"I'm glad you finally stepped out and started dating again," Deacon said. "For a moment, I thought Thandie still had you in a headlock."

I jerked my head back while twisting my mouth at his low-key shade.

"Nobody has me in a headlock, man. I told you I've been done with Thandie, although she still has a few things left at the house.. and has the key…"

My words trailed off as I realized that I, in fact, looked like Thandie still had me in a death grip. To add insult to injury, Deacon veered back and screeched, "The key, my dude!!"

Deacon propped his hand on his leg and tilted his head to the side, adding more dramatics as he questioned, "Nigga, you can't completely move on until she gets the rest of her stuff and give you the key back. You know she planted those boxes there as a way to still stake her claim on you, right?"

I nodded slowly, acknowledging the truth behind why those boxes were still there. I knew all along that she just so happened to leave those boxes for other reasons she didn't speak of, but it wasn't doing her any good because I wasn't even thinking about dating anyone until now. Could I even consider myself dating Nina? It was only one dinner date, but I couldn't deny I was interested in seeing her again.

"You gotta get that closed out before it gets too deep with Nina," Deacon warned.

"Too deep?" I asked, huffing a short laugh. "We only went on one date."

"Yeah, one date, but the way you're over there smirking and getting all googly-eyed talking about her, it's fitna be another date... *and* another. You know how you roll, Romeo."

"Aight, man," I said, sucking my teeth. I took the towel on the floor and whipped it towards him. "You're going to stop talking about me like I'm some kind of lovesick puppy or something."

Deacon grabbed the end of the towel and snatched it from my hands with a chuckle. "Not a lovesick puppy, but an abiding dog...once he got a nice little tail he's following around."

"Aight, man, whatever," I cracked up, and so did Deacon.

"Look, my lady got me going to this candle-making joint this weekend. It's a wick-and-sip situation. You should see if Nina wants to join for a double date."

The thought of double dating with Deacon's loud, outspoken ass had me ready to decline. Allowing Deacon to say something crazy about me didn't appeal to me, but the opportunity to see Nina again did. Granted, we've had light text conversations over the last few days since our date, but it didn't compare to seeing her face again. I wanted to see her pretty face again.

"I'll see what she says," I agreed. Deacon and I got up and dapped, ready to end our gym session.

Nine

Nina

Before I descended the last flight of steps to the ground floor of my apartment building, I stopped and did a once-over of myself. Here I was, getting ready to go on my second date with Denzel, and I was questioning my outfit moments before seeing his face again. Most of my fretting was because it wasn't just a date with him but a double date with his friends. I was already going to meet his friends, and I wasn't sure how to feel about that. Not that I was going to turn away and ditch the date. It was just...different. A good kind of different. It felt good to have Denzel interested in me enough to want to introduce me to his friends.

I mentally kicked away my useless doubt about my appearance. I loved the dress I picked, my favorite summer number: a mid-thigh white and burnt orange floral dress. It gave a bodice at the top with thin straps and then flared out just past my hips, giving my petite frame an extra boost and bang. I paired it with a pair of orange open-toe slip-on heels—made for walking with its chunky two-inch heels. I let out a breath and shrugged as I took the final steps. *This is it.*

Denzel insisted that he would come to the door, but I opted for him not to. Although impressed with his chivalry, I needed a moment to fret over myself without him being a witness. I had to shake out my nerves and let out a couple of "woos," all in an attempt to be normal. This was my first time seeing him since he came over. It was the first time I saw him outside of *my dreams*. Those dreams of him plagued me for a few nights this week, probably because we communicated quite a bit through text. The more I talked to him, the more I liked him, and the more my body reacted in ways it shouldn't be for this very new man in my life. When I stepped on the leveled ground and saw him standing on the passenger side of a new model Jeep Wrangler, my heart flipped, and my knees weakened without fail. See, this is what I mean by my body reacting in wild ways over this man.

His smile greeted me first, then his broad arms wrapped around my waist loosely in a friendly hug. I fell into it, along with the allure of his tobacco and vanilla scent. I've smelled this scent before, but it smelled delicious on him.

"You look beautiful," he complimented, opening the passenger door. His words sent a warm flutter through me, and I couldn't help but smile. He offered his hand for me to take as I stepped into the jeep.

Still standing at the door, I took in Denzel's appearance. He was wearing a white short-sleeved button-down and khaki shorts. His shirt buttons were unbuttoned just enough to show off the pronounced curves of his upper chest and a modest gold link chain. He looked handsome, and I couldn't help but admire him.

My eyes glided up to his gaze, and I softly enamored, "Thanks. You don't look bad yourself."

Denzel winked before shutting the door, the wink hitting me square in the chest. I watched as he strolled in front of the Jeep to the driver's side, getting in. As the truck's engine purred, the sounds of N.E.R.D's "Run to the Sun" glided through the speakers.

Nina

"So you like mythology *and* spaceships?" I joked, playing on N.E.R.D.'s spaceship vibes.

He chuckled as he pulled off and confessed, "I am a bit eccentric regarding my interests."

"I like it," I quickly said, dispelling any thought that I was teasing. We made eye contact briefly before I moved my eyes forward and placed my thoughts and words back on the music. "N.E.R.D. is a nice vibe. Perfect for the beachy vibes of Lovey's Bay. I bet you like anime too, don't you?"

"Damn, you're reading me, huh?"

"No!" I said quickly, my eyes widening.

Denzel's laugh was infectious, and I joined in, realizing he wasn't taking offense. He admitted, "I do watch a little of it. The concepts are pretty cool. Do you watch?"

I looked ahead at the blur of the city as we cruised through, thinking of how I had only watched a few because of Pierre. I opted not to admit that and said, "No, I don't."

He hummed, and silence fell between us as we immersed ourselves in the sound of the music, which changed to something with a little more of an island vibe. I recognized that we were heading to a small artsy area outside the Lovey's Bay boardwalk, which we affectionately called the Art Walk. The area featured a small art exhibit hall and an array of local artisan shops within a two-block radius of the region. I assumed we were going to Wick & Wine, a local candle-making shop that held a Couples Night twice a month. The cute space opened just months before Pierre and I broke up. Needless to say, we didn't make it there, and I never made plans to go, not even for the Ladies' Night.

Denzel parallel parked a few stores down from Wick & Wine and helped me out of the Jeep. The block was busy with patrons, as expected on a Friday evening. We weaved our way through coupled and single individuals with the scent of frankincense, myrrh, and lemongrass leading the way to the Wick & Wine storefront. We were met by one of the firefighters who accompanied Denzel to my last near-emergency incident and his date. When the tall, husky man's eyes met mine with a familiar look, my stomach twisted with slight embarrassment. He moved his gaze from me to Denzel when we approached and dapped him.

"My man," his voice thundered when he greeted Denzel. "On time as usual."

"You know me, Deac. Always on time, never late," Denzel quipped with a proud smile. He placed a hand on the small of my back as he stepped back to bring me more into view. "Deacon, Vanessa, this is Nina. Nina, this is my Captain, Benjamin Deacon, but we call him Deacon, and his fiancee, Vanessa."

Deacon took my hand and nodded. "I remember you. Are you taking it easy in that kitchen?"

My smile quivered as my embarrassment rose from my stomach to my cheeks. Deacon moved his eyes to Denzel, prompting me to glance and see a grimacing look on his face. This caused another wave of embarrassment to run through me. The full-figured beauty, Vanessa, saved the moment.

"Benny, leave this girl alone. You can't even boil water," she said, giving him a side-eye and pursing her lips. She stepped before a gawking Deacon, shooting a teasing wink as she took me into a warm hug. Her hug smelled like citrus and powder, wrapping me in comfort. "Nice to meet you, Nina."

"Nice to meet you, too," I responded, steadying my smile as we parted.

"I was just playing, Nessa," Deacon whined to Vanessa before turning to me. "I'm sorry if I offended you, Nina."

Deacon chuckled but held sympathy in his eyes. He bounced his gaze from Vanessa to me. Vanessa pursed her lips at him as she returned to his side, and he wrapped his arms around her waist.

"It's okay, no offense taken. I know my struggles," I said, making light of the joke and chuckling a little.

Vanessa threw her hand playfully my way. "Honey, we all struggle with something. I got you if you want a lesson or two."

"Yeah, my thickums can throw down," Deacon cooed, squeezing Vanessa as he smooched her cheek. She giggled at his affection.

I smiled at their public display, taking in Deacon's evident admiration for Vanessa. Deacon was a tall and stout man whose pecan complexion glowed from his bald head to his jolly face. He towered over Vanessa, but from Vanessa's sass and confidence, you could tell he was a teddy bear when it came to her. They had that old-school kind of love vibe where there were no doubts if he loved his woman down because he showed it in everything he did, like the way he pulled the heavy wooden door open and placed his palm in the small of her back as she sashayed in.

Denzel grabbed the door after Deacon followed Vanessa in and held it open for me. My insides heated at his chivalry and then combusted when I felt his hand graze the small of my back before it found comfort at my shoulder blade. I wouldn't have opposed his hand finding comfort in the dip of my back, though.

The old rowhouse-turned event space was comfortably filled with couples seated at their tables, serenaded by neo-soul music playing through the speakers intricately situated throughout the room. It gave me a real vibey mood that I quickly relaxed in now. The hostess had already greeted Deacon and Vanessa when Denzel and I crossed the threshold and led the way to our candlelit table, ducked away in a corner just a ways from a cherrywood staircase. Another hostess came to the table, offering glasses of wine.

"Peach," Denzel and I said in unison when asked about our choice of wine, prompting us to steal glances and stunned smirks at each other.

"Look at y'all, turning into Double Mint twins already," Vanessa teased, her big smile shining so bright that her quick wink almost went unnoticed.

The thought of being in sync with Denzel like this caused me to bite on the inside of my mouth, trying to control a blush, fighting for freedom. I was glad how quickly the hostess returned with our wine selections, and we toasted to a fun night and fell into light banter. Through our conversations, I learned that Denzel and Deacon went through Fire Academy and worked their way up the ranks together. I also learned that Deacon and Vanessa had been engaged for the last two years, and she subtly expressed her discontent with that fact.

"Mmhmm, *two years*," Vanessa emphasized as she looked at me with her round eyes even bigger. The soprano of Tevin Campbell's voice flowed in the background when she narrowed them slightly and glanced at Deacon. "He's gonna be croonin' and beggin' like Tevin for me to talk to him if he doesn't get it together."

My eyes grew big as my mouth formed an "O," and Denzel and Deacon cracked up at Vanessa's threat.

"I ain't laughin'," Vanessa warned, pursing her lips and folding her arms.

Deacon's laugh faltered as he whined, "Nessa, c'mon. You know I'm gonna marry you—"

"Uh-huh, you say that, but here are two years post-engagement."

The hostess saved Deacon momentarily as she called for the room's attention. Denzel and I exchanged looks of amusement at Vanessa's winning swordplay and gratitude that Deacon didn't have to get pistol-whipped by Vanessa's words anymore. He mouthed "sorry" to me, and I quickly dismissed his apology. I was relieved that my cooking was not the subject of conversation. We tuned in to the hostess' spill just as she explained the contents of the two open-backed bookcases pushed together and in the middle of the room. They held small fragrance bottles, one masculine scented and the other feminine scented oils.

Nina

When it was our time to choose our fragrances, I had no idea what I wanted for my candle, but Denzel's tobacco scent inspired me to select a teakwood. I walked around to the opposite side to peruse the assortment of feminine scents for a musk, a favorite powdery note. When I came across Egyptian musk, I quietly gasped with joy. I twisted the top off and put the bottle to my nose. My eyes closed as I inhaled the heavenly scent and decided it was the second note for my candle. When I opened my eyes, Denzel stood opposite, peering at me through the shelves.

Butterflies took over my stomach as I fell into his piercing gaze. He looked at me with a wonder that prickled the skin on the back of my neck and held me captive. I wondered what it was about me that caught his attention and what about him I felt so drawn to. I blinked away from his pupils, only to land on his lips. I licked my lips at the thought of licking them. *They look delicious...*

"Are you finding everything okay?"

I was startled out of my thoughts by a smiling assistant.

"Yeah, I-I am, thanks. I think I'm going to go with just these two scents," I said, quickly securing the top of the Egyptian musk and striding back to our table.

When I returned, Vanessa was seated at the table, organizing her fragrances. She looked up, happy to see me.

"Nina! Come sit. Let's chat."

I smiled nervously, unsure what we would chat about.

She leaned into me after I sat in my seat and said in a low voice, "I'm sorry for all my mess with Deacon earlier. It's just when we start talkin' about this engagement; it throws me all in a tissy."

I shook my head quickly. "No, no need to apologize. I get it. Two years is a long time."

"Tuh, tell me about it. But enough about me and my big baby Deacon. How long have you and Denzel been seeing each other?"

"Well," I started, apprehensively playing with my oils while I tried to decipher what exactly Denzel and I were doing. "I wouldn't say we are seeing each other. This is like our second date."

She scrunches her nose and questions, "Really? The chemistry between the two of you gives off longer."

"You think so?" I asked. A confused smile crossed my face as I looked toward where Denzel and Deacon were standing and talking, then back to her. I felt the spark between us, but I was surprised that Vanessa could pick up on it, too.

She nodded slowly with a cheesy grin.

"Yes. It's the way y'all look at each other." She fanned herself and giggled. "I've known Denzel by the way of Deacon for a long time. He's a good man. The last girl he dated, I could tell he really liked her. He looked at her like he looks at you, but as for her, she didn't give off the same vibe. With you two, I can tell you two are really feeling each other. Hold on to your rod tight, honey; don't let that good catch go."

Vanessa nudged me playfully as we giggled at her remark, but my mind was buzzing. She gave me a lot of information in one dialogue and a little insight into Denzel's past that had me curious to know more.

Ten

Denzel

I knew linking up with Deacon and Vanessa would be a scene straight out of a telenovela, and I was right. They were hot and tipping to cold all night, recovering barely with Deacon's sweet nothings. Whenever they seemed to be getting ready to make a hard left, I glanced at Nina. Well, not just because of them. Nina was breathtaking. But yeah, part of the reason was definitely to make sure she was not ready to ditch the date because of them. Each time, though, I found that we were in synch and ended up looking at each other at the same time. Her cinnamon eyes never showed discomfort, though. Her eyes showed what felt like the same wonder I held for her.

I was relieved when we parted ways for the evening, with Nina and I deciding to stroll the boardwalk.

"I know Deac and Vanessa can be a bit much," I skirted into my apology once we were far away and in the opposite direction from the pair.

She glanced at me, scrunching her button nose before waving off my apology.

"Pssh. It was fun being around them. I enjoyed meeting them and getting some deets about you."

"Oh, is that right?" I asked. My mouth fell open as I huffed a soft chuckle at her revelation.

She smirked, and with a slow nod, she deliberately shifted her focus to the path before us.

"Yep. I learned a lot from Vanessa."

Surprised at the culprit of the information, my laughter broke through the air as I asked, "What? What did Vanessa have to tell you about me?"

We walked silently for a beat. I looked at Nina, and she was wearing a straight face. I bunched my eyebrows in confusion and placed my hands in my pockets, and then another beat passed. After the third and glancing over to her to find she was still holding a straight face, my heart started pounding for a way out of my chest. My mind was racing through my history, trying to figure out what she could've told her. Nina moved her eyes to me and then burst into laughter. No, it wasn't a laugh. It was a sound that combined wheezing and snorting.

"You should've seen your face!" Nina grappled in between her wheezy, snorting laugh.

I stopped in my tracks and looked at her with amusement. Amusement of this weird ass laugh that was coming out of this beautiful being.

"No, you should hear yourself. Do you hear yourself? Where did this laugh come from?"

Nina's eyes bugged out as if she was shocked at herself or perhaps me, and then the laugh went wild again, this time sounding like a Volkswagen's horn and backfired by a snort. I couldn't help but laugh at this newfound sound coming from her. Nina clasped her hands over her mouth, trying to stifle the sound, leaving a hyperventilating snort to be heard. As odd as the laugh was, it was cute. She was cute.

"Oh my God, I can't believe I let that come out," she mused between calming breaths. She covered her mouth again, trying to keep her growing laughter at bay.

Instinctively, I pulled her hand from her mouth and pulled her into a hug. I mumbled into her hair, "Don't hide it. I heard it now. It's cute."

Nina's laugh faded into a titter as her arms hesitated and then wrapped around my waist. For a moment, I got lost in the feeling of having a woman so close to me, having a woman's powdery scent engulfing me. And then I got lost in that it was Nina, and it felt right to embrace her, to have her pressed against my chest, our rapidly beating hearts finding sync. But then I realized the boundary I had crossed and relaxed my grip around her shoulders.

I pulled away physically while trying to reel my mind back in with the movement, but when my orbs met her glowing, enraptured eyes, I was malted lava. Not wanting to, but needing to, I broke our gaze with a forced seeping of air through my lips as I placed my eyes on the ice cream stand a few short steps away from us. A perfect way to cool off these feels.

I stepped away slightly, letting my right-hand trail down to her left. To my surprise, she interlocked her tiny hands into mine, and I gently secured the hold. My heart imploded. I looked at our hands momentarily, mine a giant to hers. Hers provided a feminine touch to the view with her nails red-manicured and shaped, her fingers adorned with a few subtle gold rings on her thumb, index, and pinky finger. I met her eyes again and smiled as she bashfully looked down and tucked away a short curl.

"Ice cream?" I asked, breaking the heated silence.

She looked up again and bit her lip. I wasn't sure if it was her suppressing excitement or an act of contemplation. Her bottom lip slid through her teeth into a big smile as she squealed, "I thought you'd never ask."

I exhaled a laugh and led the way to the ice cream stand. Stopping

Smoke Signals

before the attendant, I nodded to her to place her order first. I watched her intently eye the menu while she mindlessly traced her bottom lip with her finger, absorbing her cute quirks. Her eyes bubbled as she pointed at her choice.

"Mm, I'll take the Maple Vanilla ice cream with the bacon bits. In a cup, please."

"And you, sir?" I heard the young attendee ask, my gaze still resting on Nina. She looked up at me, catching me admiring her. This startled me into a chuckle as I focused on the menu before us as if I needed to ponder the selections. I ordered what I always ate when it came to ice cream.

"Cookies and cream, please. In a cup."

The attendee went to work with our orders.

"I didn't take you to be a cookies and cream kind of guy," Nina said, raising her right brow and forming her face into an expression of gaiety.

"I didn't take you to be a Maple Vanilla Bacon Bits kind of girl," I countered back, curving my lips into a half smile.

She released a light-hearted chuckle and took her mountain of vanilla ice cream oozing maple syrup from the attendee. Immediately, she scooped a small layer of ice cream with her spoon and wrapped her lips around it. I licked my lips as if chasing after that spoon for a taste of her. Pulling the spoon from her mouth, she admitted, "I've never had it. New experiences kind of night."

"And here's your ice cream, sir."

I turned to the young man holding out my ice cream, exchanging the cup with a bill big enough to cover the two ice creams and a nice tip for him. He excitedly thanked me, and I lifted my head to his gratitude before we continued down the boardwalk.

We walked silently for a spell, both enjoying the ice cream and the lull of the waves crashing onto the now almost dark beach. The street lights lining the boardwalk gave a sun-like effect, lighting up the way. Even though it was nearly nine at night, the boardwalk was still decorated with people, many being couples and a few late-night joggers and bikers. It was Nina who broke the silence.

"Vanessa didn't say anything bad about you. She actually said a lot of good things…, like …that your last girl let go of a good catch."

"Hmm," I hummed, stretching my eyebrows up at the information Vanessa was forthcoming with. Not knowing what Vanessa said about my last relationship, yet not wanting to dig for the answer, I responded with four short words, "That's good to know."

It fell silent between us again, and I could only assume that Nina was waiting for me to expound on what Vanessa meant about my last relationship. I've avoided discussing Thandie for some time, mostly because I just wanted to move past the disappointment of the wasted time. But avoiding has done nothing but literally keep the door open for her to pop her head in to see what I'm doing and still hold stakes on space in my life. I had an itch to get to know Nina better, and I knew that diving into our past relationships would be a part of it. Thanks to Vanessa, that conversation would happen sooner than I wanted.

But not yet. I was saved from elaborating with the giant sight of the Lovey's Bay Ferris Wheel in front of us. After finishing the last of my ice cream and tossing it into a nearby waste bin, I turned to Nina, who was still nursing her ice cream as she gazed with big eyes at the city's staple attraction.

"Want to get on?" I asked, wiggling my eyebrows. Her beautiful smile brightened again as she turned to me and nodded.

There wasn't much of a line at this time of night, so we eased through the metal gates and were helped into the encapsulated seating. Nina slid in first, and I ducked in, sitting beside her, figuring it would provide us more space and me the opportunity to be close to her. Moments later, upbeat island music began playing, and the wheel moved us up into the night sky. Nina continued to enjoy her ice cream while I pondered whether to address the topic of Thandie.

"How long have you and your ex been apart?" Nina asked.

Well, the decision was made.

"Uh, four months," I dragged but quickly elaborated. "It's been over longer, though."

"What does that mean?"

Here we go.

"I knew the relationship wasn't going anywhere for some time. We wanted different things. I wanted to settle down and get married. She gave me the run around about that type of commitment."

She hummed her short response. When she said nothing, I looked at her. She looked like she was in her thoughts, her spoon resting between her lips. The abrupt stop of the Ferris wheel broke her from her trance and sent me on high alert. I peered through the window to find we were at the highest point. After a few moments of scanning, it didn't appear to be anything wrong. The music continued to play.

I looked back at Nina, whose eyes were on me, looking for answers. I smirked and reassured her, "Looks like it's just a routine pause. Nothing to worry about."

"Good." Her voice was softer than usual, and the following chuckle gave off a slight sadness. I could tell that whatever was on her mind after I told her about my relationship with Thandie was still plaguing hers. I was curious if it had anything to do with her past.

"What happened with your last relationship?" I probed.

She looked up at me as she heard my question with a slight shock, similar to my reaction to having to talk about my own past. She looked down at her surprisingly still intact last scoop, picking at it with her spoon.

"It's kinda similar to yours, but I was the one who wanted to settle down. I thought we'd get married, too, except he ended things with no real reason six months ago. Not too long ago, I found out he was engaged."

I whistled, feeling the blow of finding out that kind of news. To think I thought my situation was fucked up. Nina's topped mine and I wasn't proud of that. Nina was sweet, funny, and beautiful. It baffled me to hear that a man couldn't see she was wife material, or even better, worth an explanation of why his dumb ass was walking away. Hearing that he was already engaged gave off the impression he had already moved on before they officially broke up. Fuck boy shit.

I gently tapped Nina's leg, getting her attention. I deadpanned on her and declared, "I hope you know that shit he pulled had nothing to do with you. A man knows what he wants from the start, always. He was just in the way of a real one coming into your life."

My words held so much weight, so much of the truth I was feeling about her, and I hoped she caught it. The way her eyes softened and entrapped me again, I could tell she did. It was getting harder with every gaze to resist tasting her lips, especially as I watched her mindlessly take another scoop of her ice cream, anticipating her lips' retrieval.

A jolt of the machine causes us to both buck forward. I steadied myself and looked to Nina, ready to ask if she was okay, but found myself tightening my lips not to laugh. I could not laugh at the mishap of the milky ice cream splattered in a "nutty" kind of way on her forehead. She scrunched her brows, unsure how to make out my expression, and then broke into a cheesy smile, causing me to break my character.

She shook her head and shrugged, joining my cackle with her wild honky-snort, which caused me to howl. She covered her mouth, stifling her laugh.

"What, Denzel?! What's so funny?"

I could *not* tell her. I would *not* tell her. The last thing I wanted to do was make her feel awkward or embarrassed. Instead, I took my thumb and swiped the residue from her forehead. She gasped as her cheeks turned rosy. With one swipe, I took my tongue to my thumb and licked the sweet and salty residue of her ice cream.

I furrowed my brows and twisted my mouth into a grin. "Damn, this is actually good!"

I looked back at Nina. Her eyes were holding what looked like lust, but in a split second, she faltered into embarrassment. She slumps her head down and slaps the place where the ice cream once resided.

"Oh. My. God. Did I have a 'Something About Mary' moment?" she groaned.

I roared, thinking about the infamous scene, which did not help Nina's feelings at all. Seeing the pout take over her face softened my heart. I wrapped my arm around her shoulder, pulled her into me, and planted an endearing kiss on her forehead. I wasn't completely aware of my actions until I looked down at her. Meeting her heavy eyes, I was fully aware when I kissed her again. This time, I took what I wanted—her lips.

Eleven

Nina

The door swung open, causing the door knob to bang loudly against the adjacent wall as we stumbled across the threshold. Lips glued, we waltzed a half circle until my back was towards the door. I frantically waved my hand to find the doorknob while Denzel held me to his body. Finally, making contact with the cold knob, I gave it a swift swing before wrapping my arms around Denzel's neck and my legs around his waist as he hoisted me up to meet his eye level. I collided with the door, and as it clicked shut, I released a gaspy moan as he trailed kisses down my chin to my neck.

They say forehead kisses are universally the most intimate kisses. For the spiritual, a forehead kiss touches the third eye, the portal to vision or seeing one's inner thoughts. To the romantic, it expresses care, sending signals of tenderness, warmth, and closeness. For me, all of the above was the correct answer to what spurred after Denzel's forehead kiss. He saw me. I saw him. We saw each other. And what I believed we saw in each other's smoldering gazes was the steaming smoke signal that we both wanted each other. Badly.

That forehead kiss became the most tender kiss I felt in a long time. Mariah Carey's 'Fantasy' queued in my head as I finally indulged in his lips. It's a weird song choice, but it felt right, being on the Ferris wheel in this romantic moment with all of my fantasies of Denzel over the last couple of weeks rushing to the forefront. His thoughts weren't far off because, from how he kissed me, it felt like he had been waiting for this moment, too. The exploration of tongues with each other's mouths didn't end until we heard the rapping of the Ferris wheel attendee on the door. We tried to collect our composures and carry on like the moment didn't happen. We were successful with this act all the way to my apartment door.

We shared a quick peck before saying good night, although I wasn't so sure I wanted the night to end. I pondered this as I fumbled with my keys to unlock the door. I heard the click of the door unlocking and pushed the door ajar but paused.

Fuck it. YOLO.

When I turned around to make my move, Denzel's bouldering body accosted me, and I just melted into him—into his lips, into his touch. That's how I ended up here, sandwiched between Denzel and the door, being freed from the shackles of my dickless life.

Denzel let out a low growl as he sucked with a gentle yet firm pressure on my neck, eliciting a whimpered moan from me. My pussy quaked at the sound of his feral call. I was ready to answer. He spun us around as if we were performing a forbidden dance. For me, this was a forbidden dance. I was not supposed to be entangled in another man just yet. This time was for me. For me to give myself self-love…

Self-love is also getting some lovin', bitch! Get it…get it!

"Do you want to stop?" Denzel panted, placing me on the tufted arm of the couch. He kissed my lips again before attempting to search my pupils through the street light that shined through the dark room.

Even in the room's darkness, I could see the hunger in his eyes. I was

Nina

set ablaze and wanted nothing but him to simmer my fire. Even with my mind racing with every reason not to continue, I whispered, "No," and opened my legs a little more, inviting him to move in closer.

We continued to kiss feverishly, taking turns sucking on each other's lips. My head fell back as he placed his hand on the back of my neck and took languid licks and kisses down. Tingles ran through nerves I didn't know were in my body as he adored my neck. I sucked in a breath and bit on my lip as he freed one hand from my waist and cupped my breast, kneading it through the fabric of my dress. The friction quickly caused my nipple to pebble.

Wanting to feel his full lips against mine again, I cupped his face, guiding him back to my face. He obliged my subtle want for another kiss as I wrapped my arms around his neck again, this time for support as I rocked into him, letting my legs fall open more. I had no idea what had gotten into me, but I didn't care. I was in the middle of one of my fantasies, and I wanted to see it through.

Denzel's hands ventured up my bare thighs and under the skirt of my dress. I shivered at the feel of his pads pressed into my thighs and gliding up to the sides of my ass. I didn't have much, but Denzel gripped what I had like it was a wagon before trailing his hands back down my thighs in a massaging motion, still tonguing me down. The pulsing between my legs was knocking now, wanting Denzel to enter.

"I can stop," he whispered before nibbling on my ear.

"No, don't stop," I moaned, massaging the back of his neck. "Keep… going."

"Can I go….here?"

He trailed his finger over the seat of my lace panties and inhaled a shaky gasp. My mind was sending off alarms and shouting no, but my body…my body wanted this more than anything.

"Mmhmm," I hummed and nodded lazily as he made circles around my button through the lace material.

My breaths grew deep and released as pleasurable whimpers with every circle around my clit. My essence collected in the seat of my panties. My love below vibrated with anticipation for...

I gasped audibly as I arched my back in response to his finger sinking into my center and pulling out my wetness.

He groaned into my mouth, "You're so....wet...Goddess."

There he goes with the Goddess again, causing me to spill even more on the finger that stroked my insides, deep and in a slow, deliberate motion. And then, he furthered my pleasure, stretching me with the addition of another finger. I whimpered at the feel of him slowly stroking me to oblivion.

I kissed him deeper and pulled him closer, wanting his fingers deeper. He received my subtle message, cupping my neck with his free hand to thrust his tongue deeper into my mouth as he thrust deeper and harder inside my sex. I was no longer there on the edge of my couch, being finger-fucked. I was on a cloud, and his fingers were his dick, thrusting and stroking and thrusting, and I was falling into the clouds...

"Ahh...Oh...My...Goood—"

My orgasm came out through short pants and then a whimper. My body exploded like it was the Fourth of July, and fireworks were going off in my pussy. When I opened my eyes, I found myself not falling off a cloud but backward onto the couch, legs flailing, and then falling into my center table. To Denzel's defense, he tried to break my fall, only for me to grab hold of the neck of his shirt and take him down with me.

Oh, Nina...what a way to orgasm.

Twelve

Nina

I just knew my acrobatic orgasm would've turned Denzel away. I don't know why I couldn't keep my uncoordinated behaviors at bay in front of this man. Honestly, I wouldn't have even been mad if he decided to ghost me and never look back; it would make it so much easier for me to get my focus back on my Moments of Yes. Back to me. But, for whatever reason, the Universe had something else planned. Denzel called me the next day, and the next, and then the next. Then, our weekly dates became standing weekly dates, and here we are, a month later, prepping for game night with Joni and Tevin.

Yes, Tevin, the firefighter with all the jokes the day I met Denzel. Considering Joni's reservations around his age, I don't know how this became a thing, but here we are. It was an easy decision to invite them over for game night. With us both knowing the pair, it called for a night to be fun. At least, I hoped so. This was my first time seeing Tevin since my fire accident, and I was hoping he was over the jokes now that we were months past it.

"I told him not to bring it up. And if he does, I'm gonna sic Deacon on his ass," Denzel reassured me when I grumbled my hopes not to have my cooking disaster left behind. To my defense, I have actually gotten better since Denzel has been around. A few of our date nights involved us staying in and cooking something new together.

We were standing in the kitchen, arranging a couple of trays of chips and dip. I looked over at him with eyebrows sketched in inquiry. I chuckled before asking, "Sic Deacon on him?"

He met my eyes as he placed the tub of dip in the middle console of the tray. "Yeah, they are always roasting at the station, and Deacon always wins. He doesn't want that upset this week."

We both laugh at the thought of Deacon and Tevin battling it out with jokes. I didn't know Deacon well, but I definitely learned he was slick with his mouth from our double date.

The zesty and enticing smell of the combination of tomato sauce, mozzarella cheese, and Italian seasoning from the homemade pizza we were baking pleasantly assaulted my nose, causing me to glide toward the oven to take a peek. "Mmm, the pizza smells so good."

"Aht aht, don't touch that oven just yet," Denzel ordered, catching my hand and spinning me into his arms. "It still has some baking to do. My lips are hot and ready for you, though."

I tightened my lips over my grin before our lips met, pecking first and then falling into a languid kiss. My heartbeat dropped down to my love below, ready to rev my girl up. I inhaled a sobering breath and pulled away from his kiss. He protested my backing away with a slow shake of his head as he pulled my bottom lip back between his lips, sucking gently. The suction on my lip pulled a soft moan out of me as I parted them, welcoming his warm tongue into my mouth.

God, he's going to make me reconsider my stance on taking things slow… again.

Remembering my initiative to take a step back and slow the fire between Denzel and me, I reluctantly pulled away from our liplock again. I gently put my hand on his hard chest to create some distance. "We have to take it slow," I said, my words airy.

He nodded, giving my waist a little squeeze. "Okay. Does that mean I can't kiss you?"

"No," I quickly sing. Just as much as he enjoyed kissing me, I enjoyed kissing him. "It's just a reminder."

"Fair. I'll wait for you," he murmured. He pressed his bottom lip between his teeth before releasing it into a devious grin. "But I won't wait for another kiss."

I huffed out a laugh, holding my mouth open to say something, but fell short as Denzel went in for another kiss. This time, I didn't think of any of my reservations. I just savored the kiss.

It wasn't like I didn't want to have sex with Denzel. Hell, we've had a form of it already, but I think my electrifying orgasm zapped some sense into me. Maybe not some sense, but some reserve. Was I moving too fast? Was I abandoning my intentions of finding myself for a man again?

It was like the orgasm reminded me of all the reasons why I fell for Pierre and why it didn't work. *Perhaps I gave him too much too fast without knowing if we were truly on the same page. Maybe I didn't spend enough time learning what I wanted.*

I liked Denzel, but I didn't want to make the same mistakes again, so I suggested we slow things down sexually. As far as kisses, I wanted them. I needed them. It felt too good to put a pause on that. Kisses were slow, right?

Tap! Tap! Tap!

Light but firm raps to my door broke us from our make-out session. Well, me anyway. My attention went to the door, but Denzel trailed his kisses to my cheek and underneath my earlobe.

"Denzel," I whined, turning my head to him. He took his left hand up and through my short curls, beckoning me to close my eyes as I

Smoke Signals

indulged in the pleasure of his hands on my scalp. I loved his tender touch, but I knew I would be locked in again if I stayed a minute longer. I snapped my eyes open and slid from his arms. His eyes showed his faux disappointment as I smirked and reminded him, "Our guests are here."

Our guests? I shook my head at my word choice as I walked to the door. Here I was, already staking claim and commitment on us.

The quick raps continued until I swung the door open. The knocks were coming from Joni, whom I assumed it was coming from. She stood with her fist poised to continue knocking. She released her fist and placed her open hand on her hip, the other bent and holding a bottle of wine.

Joni pursed her lips, running her tongue across her lips as she looked at me and then past me at Denzel, suspicion written all over her face. She sassed, "It took you long enough. What *y'all* doin' in here?"

I rolled my eyes. Grinning, I said, "Hello to you, too, Nosey."

"Mmhmm." Still holding her suspicious smirk, Joni sauntered past me.

Tevin stood at the door with bewilderment in his expression. He lifted his hands and shoulders and then let them drop to his side. "Damn, you just gonna leave me at the door with no introduction?"

Joni stopped and looked over her shoulder. "They know who you are, Tevin. You work with Denzel, and you've been to Nina's before, remember?"

Tevin dropped his head, shaking it as he chuckled. He looked up. "Damn, it's like that, baby?"

"It's like what? Boy, stop acting like you're brand new."

I bit down on my lip, trying to hold back my laughter. I placed a hand on Tevin's back and ushered him in. Hoping to lessen the toll of Joni's curtness, I said, "I remember you, Tevin. Come in."

"See how she do me?" Tevin asked jokingly. He looked at me with a

Nina

smirk and ambled in and towards Joni, who was placing her bottle of wine on the dining table. Placing his case of beer beside the wine, he wrapped his arms around Joni's robust hips. "I bet you won't forget my name when I have that ass—"

"Boy, if you don't stop..."

Joni swivels around to Tevin with a look of shock and a smidge of being turned on.

"Now you know I'm far from being a boy," Tevin counters, giving her ass a swift smack.

"Tevin, behave yourself!" Joni yelps and scurries away from him.

Denzel and I exchanged amused looks as he headed to the oven to retrieve the pizza that was now ready. I shrugged, not having any words for Joni and Tevin. This was Joni, through and through with her men, particularly the young men. As a matter of fact, I don't think I've ever really seen her date anyone older than her. I think she likes being in control and running the show, but from the looks of it, Tevin has what it takes to match Joni's playful sass.

A half-hour later, we were all settled in my living room, stuffed with pizza and chips. It was safe to assume that we were all enjoying a nice buzz, with Joni and I splitting the bottle of wine and the guys the beer. We carried light banter about who was dating whom in pop culture when Joni jumped in her seat.

"Oh! Speaking of dating, I bought this card game for couples. Y'all seen that page, Tonight's Conversation, on social media?"

"Yeah, I think I've seen them," I answered, looking at Denzel, who was nodding his head less confidently.

"Well, they have these card games you can play with your man, friends, or whatever. I got the one for couples and thought it would be fun," she explained as she pulled the deck of cards out of her purse and began removing them from their paper case. She paused and looked up at us. "Y'all down?"

We all agreed asynchronously, and Joni continued to explain the game. She shuffled the cards and then passed them to me, requesting that I pull a card and read the question, dare, or reward presented on it.

My eyebrows bunched, and a heatwave ran through my body as I read the dare: "Stare into your partner's eyes for 30 seconds without laughing."

"Pfft, I'm glad we didn't pull that one. Your goofy ass would've lost," Tevin joked, nudging Joni.

She rolled her eyes at him and then pointed her finger down and made a circle with it.

"Nina… Denzel, turn around and get ready. Let's see who will make it without laughing. I'm betting on Denzel."

"Damn, Joni. I thought you were my girl," I gawked, disappointed at her lack of faith in me.

"I am, but I know you." She looks up at me from her phone and sticks her tongue out at me playfully.

I turned towards Denzel, tucking my right leg under me for comfort. He turned, resting his arm on the back of the loveseat with his back against the arm. His position made his carved chest poke out, and the way his legs were spread made it hard for me to keep my eyes from falling below his waist.

"My stare game is impeccable," Denzel ticked his left eyebrow up and smirked.

I sucked my teeth and rolled my eyes playfully at him. "That's to be determined."

I inhaled and exhaled, centering my focus on the task at hand. I was determined to win. I could hear Joni counting down from 3 and then indicating that the time had started. With that, our gazes locked into place. Denzel's eyes seemed to match my determination, narrowing as mine did but then softening, causing my right eye to twitch in wonder and soften. The auburn in his pupils seemed to brighten as they dilated, becoming a portal that my orbs fell into. I believed that was what happened because my heart began to swell, and my body started tingling in a way I hadn't felt in a long time. There were feelings that I had kept tucked away from experiencing again. Feelings like liking someone deeply, adoring them, and wanting to be near and close to them all the time. I couldn't tell if they were my feelings alone or shared with Denzel, but the thought of sharing such intimate feelings with him—scared me.

"Time!"

"Damn, neither one of y'all broke. What kind of voodoo y'all got going on?"

I blinked out of the trance-like moment with Denzel and released the breath stuck in my throat, transforming it into a soft chuckle. Denzel cleared his throat, shifting in his seat as he met my eyes. I looked away, chilled and thrown by the experience.

Thirteen

Denzel

"**G**ood work tonight, folks!"

A round of tired sentiments rumbled through the station's garage as the crew filed out of the two fire trucks we just pulled back into the garage. Everyone dispersed in multiple directions. I strolled through the heavy metal door that led to the open-spaced lounge and kitchen area and then around the corner to the men's locker room and showers. Grabbing my phone from my locker, I noted the time being half past eleven at night, and still no notifications from Nina since my last message. I tapped on the Messages app, opening the thread that was once bustling with back-and-forth messages between us and zero-ing on the last blue-bubbled message I sent nearly 3 hours ago.

Denzel: When can I see you again?

I tossed my phone back into my bag and grimaced at how thirsty I felt for a response from Nina. She had me thirsty. No, correction: I have fallen into my typical pattern of letting my heart run rampant without checking to see if there was a true destination to land.

Well, I thought I had a soft place to land with Nina. We were flowing and vibing just a week ago, and there was no sign of us going from constant conversations to spotty communication. I couldn't pinpoint where things had gone wrong. Did I overstep somewhere? Did I say something wrong? Was I moving too fast?

When I got the opportunity to ask Nina what was going on, she answered that she'd just been busy with the upcoming Juneteenth event at Lovey's Bay's Farmers Market. Knowing this was true, as our company would be participating, I accepted her reasoning. Yet, my mind ran rapidly, overthinking every interaction while my heart sunk in dread, unsure which way to sway in my feelings. I knew there was something more to it than just being busy.

I grunted at the realization that I was falling back into my sunken place and busied myself with stripping down from my smoke-clad fire gear and putting it in my designated area. I stripped down from my boxer briefs and undershirt to my complete nakedness, tossed my soiled clothes in my locker, and grabbed my towel. I clunked into the shower room.

The locker room began buzzing with chatter and upbeat music, but I just wanted peace and quiet. Being in the thick of summer and the beginning of the fireworks season, our calls have increased, being especially busy today. It was good for my racing mind, keeping me from thinking about my personal life. Now that the dust had settled from today, my head was beginning to pound from the constant running of thoughts I had suppressed throughout the day. The warm water raining over my head as I ducked underneath the sprayer melted away the throbbing.

I didn't know how long I had been in the shower, but it was long enough that when I turned off the faucet, the shower room was mostly quiet besides the drip of a faucet or two. I wiped myself down swiftly and then wrapped the towel around my waist to return to the locker room, feeling less heavy than I had moments before. I sat on the bench in front of my locker and grabbed the smaller towel I had hanging. I draped it around my neck, wiping away the dripping water from my waves.

"You good, Chief?"

I looked up to find Deacon stalking towards me. He looked refreshed from his shower, sporting a T-shirt and sweats. I forced a weak smile and said, "Yeah, boss. What's up?"

"Yeah, aight," he tossed back at me, twisting his face. He stood a distance from me. "You're a quiet person, but not this quiet. What's going on at the home front?"

My eyebrows furrowed, trying to seem confused by his question, but I knew Deac saw right through me. I tried to convince him of my lie anyway. "Home front? Whatchu talking about?"

He sucked his teeth. "Last time you were like this, Thandie was giving you the runaround, and I haven't heard nothin' about a Thandie since Nina came around. So what's up?"

"I mean, nothing's really going on. It's just been a busy week," I continued with my not-so-convincing lie. I turned my eyes back to my locker, rummaging around for some clean boxer briefs.

"Hmph," Deacon hums. "Who's doing the dodging? You or Nina?"

I stepped into my boxers, dropping my towel as I pulled them up over my hips and scoffed, "Deac, man, it's not even like that, really—"

"That's not what your demeanor is showing. It's fuckin' with your head. Now, I wouldn't say anything if it wasn't a hella crazy week, but it is. And as your right hand, I gotta make sure your mind is always cleared of distractions."

I sighed heavily, knowing Deacon's prodding was of good intentions and his point valid. I've been doing well with not getting distracted, but all it takes is one distracting thought to throw your mind off of an emergency and put you at risk.

I turned and leaned on the cold locker to look at Deacon. I rubbed my damp waves and groaned before I confessed, "It's Nina. She's doing the dodging...not necessarily dodging, but she's closed off...been acting kind of weird and saying it's work. I think it's more than that, though."

He nods thoughtfully. "How long has this been going on? Y'all was just good."

"For about a week...since the game night at her house with her neighbor and Tevin."

"Tevin's the name...don't wear it out!"

Tevin rounds the corner, bopping towards us with an oblivious smirk.

"Won't nobody callin' your little ass," Deacon quipped, smacking the back of Tevin's head as he crossed and found a place beside him against the opposing lockers.

Tevin sucked his teeth and swatted at Deacon. "Aight, man, chill."

Deacon chuckled and turned his attention back to me. "Well, what could've happened at that game night to shift things with y'all?"

I shrugged lazily and shook my head. "I don't know, man. That's the same question I have."

"You talking about Nina?" Tevin asked, tilting his head. "Y'all on the outs already? Shit, I thought it would be me and Joni before you and Nina."

"We aren't really on the outs. I don't know what we are. I don't know..."

Irritated by the second round of questions, I growled and sighed all at once.

"I remember Joni saying the last dude Nina was with kind fucked her up. Dipped and ended up engaged, " Tevin shared. "She might be still dealing with that shit."

"Finally, the youngin saying something that makes sense, but you ain't had to tell all the girl's business," Deacon said, smacking Tevin on the back of the head again, causing Tevin and his head to bop forward.

Tevin balled his whole face up and grumbled, "Aight, Deac, you got one more motherfuckin' time to disrespect me like that, man! Your ol' stout ass!"

"Yeah, okay, Tevin No-Campbell," Deacon joked, belting out a hearty chuckle. I snickered at the banter myself. Annoyed, Tevin walked off and out of the locker room. Deacon turned to me. "All jokes aside, Tev got a point. If she is still dealing with heartbreak, she might've put her guard back up. "

"Yeah," I agreed, my voice trailing with my thoughts. I knew about Nina's last guy and the fucked up move he made, but I hadn't thought about her still being stuck on it. She didn't really show that she was, but it's not far-fetched.

"That kind of wall can be tough to break down and high as hell to climb. It sounds like you need to decide if she's worth the climb."

Fourteen

Nina

I looked around the grassy field filled with white tents providing cover for vendors and their tables of merchandise. Mingled in were an array of people shopping or lounging in their lawn chairs. Kids were playing like it was just them on a playground, and the uplifting tune of Sounds of Blackness's "Optimistic" floated through the humid and salty air.

Our annual Juneteenth celebration was going smoothly. I inhaled a satisfied breath and let my lips curve upwards, taking in my success in getting this thing off the ground without a hitch. I roamed over the expansive field, my eyes landing on the crew from Fire Company No. 143, and immediately found Denzel. My heart quickened at seeing him. He was dressed in a blue Fire Company No. 143 tee and slacks, his arm muscles flexing as he leaned down to adjust a fire hat on a little boy before him. A slow inhale filled my chest, followed by an even slower exhale. His fine never ceases to diminish—but that's not what I'm on right now.

Turning on my heels, I walked away, determined to keep my focus.

I would not let my agonizing desire for Denzel distract me from my mission to make Nina whole.

I'm not on that right now. I'm on making Nina whole and clear of all the things that are Pierre, I reminded myself, repeating the affirmation repeatedly in my head.

That was the sole purpose of this mental space I put myself in after game night. The feelings that I realized were bubbling up to the surface for Denzel, and the possibility that he was feeling the same scared me. I knew I wasn't ready. On top of that, every time I thought about feeling more for Denzel, Pierre came to mind. That furthered my notion that I needed to pull back, work on myself, and release the obvious hurt I was still holding on to when it came to Pierre.

Did I relay that to Denzel? No. Not really. I didn't know how to tell him that I was scared and the hurt from my past relationship was resurfacing and paralyzing me. Well, I could've told him like that. I could have told him as plainly as it formed in my head, but that seemed like a recipe for *him* to ghost me. So, instead of allowing him to ghost me, I distanced myself and kept our communication minimal and neutral. Okay, in a sense, I was on my way to ghosting him.

In my aimless effort to create even more distance from Denzel, I ran into the heels of someone.

"Oh! I'm so sorry," I quickly apologized, stepping back.

"No worries….Nina?" The familiar voice snatched my breath as I connected the voice with Pierre's face.

"Pierre…hey."

Pierre Donahue's face warmed as a grin spread across his face, igniting the dimple in his right cheek that I always melted away my senses when we were together. He still looked the same, although I didn't expect him to look much different, with only half a year passing. His fair skin was still supple and blemish-free, and his silken waved hair, mustache, and beard were crisply lined as usual. Pierre was a pretty boy through and through.

When my eyes focused on the tall, model-esque woman by his side, my heart hit the bottom of my stomach, realizing this was the said fiancee. She was beautiful, wearing her long dark hair in body waves, her slinky dress draping her elegantly. She smiled at me, showcasing pearly white teeth and happiness—happiness that mimicked the happiness Pierre used to bring out of me.

"I didn't expect to run into you," Pierre continued. My eyes darted to him, narrowing slightly as anger ran through me. I forced a tight smile as he turned to the woman hanging from his arm. "Nina, uh, this is..my fiancee, Dana."

"Nina," she mused in a light soprano thick with an island accent. She stretched her manicured hand out to shake. The sparkling princess-cut diamond caught my eye. "It's nice to meet you," she said.

"Nice to meet you, too, Dana," I lied, shaking her hand before nervously tucking a short curl behind my ear.

I looked back at Pierre, who seemed to struggle with his words. Hell, I was struggling with what to say next or if I should even say anything at all. I could feel the water lining my eyes and my pulse racing. All I knew was that between dodging Denzel and bumping into Pierre and his fiancee, it was all too much for me.

I blinked rapidly, whisking the tears away before shortening the awkward introductions. "Well, it was nice running into you, Pierre. Dana. I have to get back to work."

I spun on my heels, briskly walking back in the direction I was avoiding, not waiting for Pierre or Dana to say anything. I just wanted out of their presence, away from the reminder of my past. My damn thoughts manifested this. I shook my head quickly, placing a hand on my temple to massage away the frustration as the other swung back and forth with my brisk walk. I was jerked out of my inner scolding by a masculine hand catching mine.

"I've been trying to catch up with you."

My misty pupils met with Denzel. A sense of comfort mixed with dread washed over me—so many emotions in less than five minutes. I took a deep breath, attempting to clear the feelings of seeing Pierre brought up, but it only reminded me that those very feelings were why I was avoiding Denzel.

"Denzel. Hey, I've been—"

"Busy," he completed my sentence. A melancholy smile crossed his face before his eyes narrowed with concern. "Are you good?"

I blinked rapidly again, willing away my emotions. "Yeah, yeah. It's just the humidity…the sun…causing my eyes to water a little."

"Do you want me to get you some water?" He asked, fully taking my hand and then stepping into full view. He took his other hand and lifted my chin so that I could look at him. I was swooning over him while in the middle of my internal chaos. Denzel scanned my face for some visible sign of distress, similar to how he looked at me the first time we met. I'm sure he could see signs of it, but most of my distress was internal and beating me up. His sincere concern for me tempted me to fall into his arms and release it all, but I stiffened, shaking my head in denial of his offer for water and denying myself my relief.

"I'll be okay. Thank you, though," I said, ripping my gaze from his. "I do have to get back—"

I looked away and attempted to pull from his grasp to head… anywhere, but he gently tightened his grasp. "Wait, Nina."

I looked at his hand gripping mine before I looked up at him. He loosened his grip slightly, rubbing his thumb across my hand.

Denzel's eyes softened, almost pleading, as he asked, "Is everything good…with us? It's just been different over the last week."

"Uh," I sighed, looking down, searching for my words…some words that would make sense. I couldn't find any, just the ones I kept feeding him. "It's just been busy… with work and—"

Nina

"Nina, it's not just work," Denzel cut through my excuse. His voice was laced with slight irritation but not raised. It was still far different than I'd heard from him, causing me to look at him. "Be honest with me, Nina. At least about that."

I couldn't blame Denzel for his frustration. I was frustrated at myself, too. *Why couldn't I just feel the good feelings and not be scared? Why can't I—*

"I just need to focus on myself right now," I blurted out, not completely aware of my words. When my mind caught up with my mouth, I realized I was in the final stretch of distancing myself from him. With everything that had just happened before, I needed to. My voice cracked as I sealed my declaration: "I need to focus on me. Get back to me. It's not you. It's me."

His usual bright eyes frosted over to gloom. Feeling my heart wrench at the hurt I caused him and myself, I slipped my hand from his and walked away.

Fifteen

Nina

My phone alarm chimed the reminder to settle whatever I was doing at nine that night and get comfortable on my balcony, just in time for the 4th of July fireworks. I just finished plating a new meal I decided to try, a creamy chicken tortellini pasta. The reddish-orange sauced pasta was still steaming, carrying the scent of the Italian herbs to my nose. My stomach growled its protest to the relaxed pace I was moving in, urging my haste to settle my debt to it. Grabbing my glass of red wine, I balanced my plate, fork, and phone in the other hand as I quickened my pace to my balcony.

The air was thick with humidity, and the smell of charred meats met my nostrils, reminding me of the holiday celebration at Lovey's Bay Beach. When asked by Joni, I passed on attending. The excessive crowd was one reason, and the other was that I wanted to continue learning to be comfortable in my skin and time. It's not like I haven't had a lot of practice with it, but, you know.

After severing what was left between Denzel and me two weeks ago, I have been immersing myself back into my initial intentions: indulging

Nina

in all the Moments of Yes that would contribute to my self-discovery and love. I got back to my cooking classes—carefully— and got back to reciting my affirmations and journaling. I focused solely on myself, and I started to feel good. My cooking was progressing. My mind was filled with positive thoughts. I felt strong and independent. But tonight, a sense of loneliness was trickling in, and I was fighting it inside.

I blew out a breath, intending to cool off my forkful of pasta but also to flutter away the feeling. The savory sauce and the oozing cheese from the stuffed pasta came through with the win, ushering in delight and pushing my loneliness aside. With each bite, my smile grew as I filled with pride in how far I had come with my cooking. I couldn't lie; Denzel's patience and tips at the beginning of my cooking journey helped make me the baby chef I am now.

Who would've thought he'd be a hell of a cook himself? Damn. I miss him.

My phone vibrating across the glass table pulled me out of my thoughts. Pulling the phone closer to me, Joni's face lit up the screen, then her hyena-like cackle when I hit the accept button and placed her on speaker.

"Hello."

"Hey, girl! Just checkin' on you. Whatcha doin'?"

"Eating," I said in between chews. The echo of the music heard from the distance and through the phone battled for precedence, causing my ears and my brain discomfort. I twisted my face and said, "Girl, it's loud. Call me back."

"Waiiit," Joni whined. "Come down and hang. Tevin won't mind."

"Nah, I'm really okay with chillin' tonight, Joni," I assured. I did not want to be a third wheel of the pair, although I was yearning for company. The roar of the crowd and Tevin being close enough to the phone that I could hear him whispering something nasty to Joni was all I needed to get off the line. "Have fun with your boo. I'll be watching from my balcony."

Smoke Signals

Joni cackled and said something to Tevin before rushing off the phone. "Okay, girl, I'll talk to you later. Bye."

Two quick beeps sounded before I could say anything, indicating that the call had ended. I chuckled, thinking about the unforeseen couple, Joni and Tevin. They weren't officially couples, but they were definitely fucking. Whatever it was to them right now, I was just happy for my girl.

I finished my dinner, took my plate back to the apartment, and returned to the balcony with the bottle of wine I started. I pulled my chair out enough to recline and propped my feet on the table. I topped my glass of wine off and placed the half-empty bottle on the floor beside me just as a quick gust of the humid air brushed over my skin. I burrowed an eyebrow at the sudden gust, but after a sip of the dry yet smooth red, the thought wandered off, and I moved on. I grabbed my phone and woke it up to find it was now a quarter to ten. I wondered why it was taking so long to start the fireworks and went to Lovey's Bay Recreations and Parks website to see if there were any updates.

@LBRecsandParks The fireworks display will begin in 15 minutes as the wind conditions should be calmer. Sit tight and get ready for the show!

The message had been posted about 10 minutes prior, and I understood the concern about the wind. The wind was very peculiar today and had played between calm and gusty the whole time. With the wind only coming in as quick, small bursts, it didn't seem like it would be a problem. I looked over to the not-so-distant beach through the bowl of my wine glass, magnifying the Ferris wheel that Denzel and I rode. The same Ferris wheel where we shared our first kiss. Like clockwork, the feels came rushing in, making my heart twist.

I opened my Message app and scrolled a little, stopping at Denzel's name. For a moment, I thought I saw three dots as if he was typing to me, and I quickly tapped on the message. When I opened it, there was no bubble indicating an incoming text. Instead, I faced his last string of messages from sometime last week.

Denzel: Hey.
Denzel: Can we talk?
Denzel: I like you, Nina. Your wall is worth the climb. Just throw the rope down to me.

My heart swelled as I read his words over again. I tapped on the screen, prompting the cursor to start blinking and waiting for me to type something. I stared at the screen, but my fingers were frozen. My words were stuck, unable to form anything legible. I couldn't reply; rather, I wouldn't let myself reply.

I have to stay here, in my space, and not let him in. I'm not ready.

That's what my mind kept repeating every time my pulse rose, anxious to feel something new—new with Denzel. I dropped the phone into my lap and squeezed my eyes shut, frustrated with this forever battle with my mind and heart. A lone tear found its way down my cheek.

"What the fuck am I doing?" I scolded myself, now finding words that I wasn't afraid to say. If only I could find the words—no—the courage to say what I really wanted to say, like how I missed Denzel's presence and wanted to be completely open with him. But that truth had a lot of fear wrapped around it, pushing it further and further from my lips.

The silent whistle of fireworks shooting off could be heard, followed by back-to-back explosions. At the sound of the boom, I submitted to my tears and my feelings—my feelings of regret, loneliness, and self-sabotage. I regretted letting those words slip from my mouth the last I saw Denzel. I regretted not being able to speak because I was so afraid to start something new. I was self-sabotaging before anything even started and was too in my head to do anything about it. The question kept running through my head: what the hell am I really doing?

A thunderous boom and crackle pulled me from my thoughts. It sounded like a firework explosion but way too close to me. I fluttered my eyes, trying to clear my vision, but a gust of wind caused me to close my eyes again. I rubbed my eyes, wiping and smearing the wetness from my eyes, still hearing the crackling of the display; however, when my vision was clear enough, I didn't see the display. I saw the adjoining apartment's roof quickly engulfed in a roaring fire.

I gasped as the whipping red and orange flames grew and spread by the second, now spreading to the roof of my apartment. My heart felt like it was lodged in my throat, beating so hard I could feel it from my chest to my head. Fire alarms were going off now, and I could hear the chatter of people below between the crackling of burning wood. I don't know how long I stood there frozen, but when I came to my senses and looked through my balcony door, I saw that the living room was beginning to fill with dark smoke, but it still appeared clear enough to escape. Stumbling from my seat, I placed my hand on the glass. With my adrenaline picking up, I slid my hand against it frantically, trying to open it, but my movements weren't faster than the flames. I felt the heat each time my hand slid against the glass. When I could finally slide the door open, I was choked by the thick smell of charred wood, and my eyes burned from the smoke. I stumbled back onto my tiny balcony, colliding with the glass table. I grasped for the table's edge, trying to stabilize myself, only to send my phone sliding across the table and off the balcony.

"Oh my God!" I screamed at the horror of losing my only form of communication. My stomach caved in as a wail spilled from my lips, and my tears spilled again. I heaved, trying to pull the air back into my body, and looked around frantically for a way to escape, but the only choice I had was to try and work my way through the smoke-filled apartment. When I whipped around, ready to sprint through the blazing room, a fiery piece of my ceiling crumbled, finding its resting place on my sofa and engulfing it in flames. I screamed and shuffled backward, bumping into the balcony table again and finding myself in a corner against the cold railing.

I was hysterically crying now, my wails echoing through the air. I couldn't see anything clearly through the flood of tears running down my face, only the fluorescent orange flames. They were bouncing and growing like those weird monster trashcans in The Wiz. That scene always scared me, and that same fear was taking over my body at that very moment. I imagined the flames dancing to me as the cans danced toward the Scarecrow. I was the Scarecrow in this scene. The only difference was that this was not a movie, and the director wasn't getting ready to shout, "Cut!" This was real life; I had nowhere to run and no one to stop this scary scene.

I'm going to die.

Sixteen

Denzel

Tevin: Where's your girl Nina? Y'all still on the outs?

I tapped out of the text thread, ignoring Tevin's question. Instead, I opened the text thread that was once active by me and Nina, staring at the three messages she never responded to. Impulsively, I typed "Happy 4th of July" but then backed spaced until there was nothing. I'd look like a sucker if I sent her a fourth message, and I wasn't sure my heart could take being left on read by her again.

I slid my phone into my basketball shorts and curled my body toward the inside of the couch. Closing my eyes, I attempted to drown out the TV on the wall of the fire station's community room and the soft chatter of the team for the night. Behind my lids, images of Nina faded in, and her last words to me.

"It's not you. It's me."

Those words haunted me, following me from Thandie's mouth and now Nina's lips, and it had me thinking, what the hell was I doing? Nina had a grip on me, and we hadn't done much besides kissing, besides the one moment I pulled a sweet orgasm from her. Because we hadn't done anything more, and I still feel this way, I knew it was something special between us. We just connected immediately. It was also why her final words to me dug into the healing wound, cracking it back open again. I didn't know where things went wrong.

Even with my eyes closed, I could sense the overhead light flickering, signaling we had an emergency call coming through. The computerized siren caused me to snap my eyes open and roll off the couch, ready to go. The monotoned, digital voice came over the speaker:

"Fire Emergency reported on 710 Loveland Court. Priority 2."

By the time the message was complete, I was already in my steel-toed boots and pants, but I paused as I secured my overall straps. The address sounded familiar. I knew the address—

"Yo, ain't that where Nina lives?"

Deacon's inquiry was like a bell chiming at a correct answer. It was Nina's apartment. Adrenaline shooting off, I moved at supersonic speed to finish getting dressed as another message came through, and another siren blared.

"Fire Emergency reported at 710 Loveland Court. Now Priority 1. Fire Emergency Report at 710 Loveland Court. Now Priority 1."

My eyes clouded over with an image of Nina in an emergency that was just classified as minimally serious to light threatening. My chest tightened as I clenched my back teeth. My ears began to ring so loud that they muted the chaos of alerts and the scattering of my team.

I blinked my eyes hard and barked my order, "Let's fucking go! Deac, you drive the engine! I got the ladder truck!"

Everything from that moment after was a blur—the road, the street lights. At that point, I was moving in pure adrenaline and muscle memory. If anyone was talking, it registered as muffled, incoherent sounds. I had one focus: get to and save Nina.

I didn't even know if it was Nina who was in danger. I just had a sinking, intuitive feeling imploding in my chest. It was the intuitive knowing you get when you know something terrible is happening. This wasn't my first rodeo, but this was my first time feeling connected to the emergency. This feeling was fucking me up on the inside, wrenching and twisting at my chest and stomach. When I stopped at the scene, I saw the angry blaze, and Nina huddled into the corner of her balcony. I could feel my heart pause and tighten in my chest.

I yanked my radio to my mouth and growled. "Incident is located at Alpha."

"Got eyes on it, boss," Deacon radios back. "Is…Is that—"

"It's Nina!"

"Fuck! Let's go, team! We got a woman on the balcony, and the fire is moving…." was the last thing I registered Deacon saying before tunneling my focus back into rescuing Nina. The continued scream of sirens played in the background as I backed the truck close to the apartment and practically hopped out. I sprinted to climb the truck to the ladder.

"Aye, Payton."

The seriousness of Deacon's tone and his calling me by my last name caused me to pause midway up. I whipped my head towards him, annoyance written all over my face.

"What?" I huffed.

"Your mental's not clear. I can go up and get her," Deacon suggested in the cool, calm tone I only hear from him when he's saying something serious.

My chest heaved up and down, unusually visible in my heavy uniform. I narrowed my eyes at him, shaking my head. "I'm the only one going up there, Deac. It's Nina—my Nina. If anyone is going to save her, it's me."

Without waiting for his response, I finished my ascend, nearly hopping the last step. Reaching the hydraulic ladder, I deployed it. I heard heavy breathing behind me and quickly peered over my shoulder to find Deacon. Turning back, I directed the ladder to Nina's balcony. The nerves in my body were undone and frazzled, anticipating the moment that the slow ascend would finally reach her balcony. There was a gust of wind that burst through the air. The fire roared and whipped as Nina shrieked. My heart was fighting to jump from my chest, and I couldn't wait any longer for the final few inches of the ladder's movement. I locked in my hat, protective eyeshield, and a mask over my mouth, scaling the steel steps with urgency.

"Nina!"

Nina snapped her head around, her almond-shaped eyes wide with horror. The wetness of her tears glistened on her face, and she was shaking. When her eyes met mine, she began to weep.

"Denzel...Denzel...you-you're here," she wailed.

I was halfway to her, but that was still too far. I sucked in a deep breath, trying to still my heart. I nodded my head, willing myself to stay professional. I assured her, "I am, Nina. I'm coming to get you."

Her erratic cries, broken by labored breaths, threatened my composure. I steadily climbed and kept repeating, "It's going to be okay, Nina," as I clacked up the fourth, the third, the second, and finally, the last step that brought me face to face with Nina. My breath was shallow, not because of the waves of heat permeating the air, but because I wanted nothing but to swoop her up like she was my Lois to my Clark.

"Nina, we have to get you off of this balcony," I instructed calmly, deadpanning on her. She heaved but quickly fell into a coughing, choking on the smoky air. I quickly looked past her at the fire now taking over her living room. "We don't have much time, Nina. What I want you to do is—"

"I'm scared," she whimpered, a fresh set of tears running from her eyes. Her words hit me in my core as if they held so much more meaning behind them, but I stayed focused on the mission.

I looked deep into her eyes, and with a steady voice, I continued to create a safe space for her.

"You're the Fire Goddess, remember, Nina?" I asked, never removing my gaze from her. She nodded quickly as a tick to the left of her mouth created an unsure smile. I continued, "You're strong, and you can do this. I'm here….right here. Remember what I said? Just give me the rope. The rope, right now, is you. Do you trust me?"

The inferno behind her crackled as she nodded slowly and then quickly. I smiled, relieved, and gave her more instructions, "Okay, I'm going to take a few steps down, and I want you to climb over the rail. I'll be *right here*. And then we'll go down together."

Nina hesitated momentarily, wiping the back of her hand across her eyes. She breathed heavily before easing herself over the railing, placing her bare feet on the metal step. She took two steps, landing in between me and the ladder rail.

Another strong breeze rushed past us, causing the skirt of her cotton dress to fly. I closed in on her, placing my heavy glove on her abdomen. She peered over her shoulder.

"I don't want you to be exposed," I explained. "I take a step, and you take a step. Got it?"

She shook her head repeatedly, and we did just that. I took a step, and she took a step, repeating until we landed on the flat roof of the fire truck and then down the final steps until we were on solid ground. I stepped off first, and before I could instruct her, she turned and fell into my arms. I hooked my arms under her legs, cradling her like a baby. She was my baby. She held her arms around my neck tightly, sobbing.

* * *

Even if Deacon hadn't volunteered to take over command, I was still going to ensure Nina was okay. Stripping from the heavy fire coat, the humid air felt like a cool springtime breeze to my sweat-clad chest. My sleeveless undershirt clung to me like a second layer of skin. Even walking briskly to the emergency vehicle Nina was in, it did nothing to dry it.

When I climbed into the ambulance, Nina was visibly calmer than before. She held an oxygen mask to her mouth and nose. Her chest rose, heavy and slowly, as her eyes lulled closed in the apparent relief and relaxation she was experiencing. She fluttered her eyes open when I slid on the bench to the left of her. A soft smile crossed her lips as I ran my hand over her frizzed curls, resisting the urge to kiss her.

She removed the mask from her face and passed it to the EMT, who sat opposite me, ensuring she was okay. I exchanged glances with the female EMT I was familiar with from past emergencies and nodded a silent assurance that I'd look out for her before she climbed out. Nina sat up a little more in her elevated position, grabbing my hand.

"Thank you, Denzel," she said softly, her eyes misting again. "I thought I was going to die up there…alone."

Her eyes grew distant within her thoughts. I squeezed her hand, bringing her back to the present moment. I looked into her eyes and declared, "Not on my watch."

She huffed out a soft chuckle and recounted softly, "You're always around to save me," she said, but then she cut her eyes towards me. "This wasn't my fault either, for the record."

"I know. Someone was shooting off fireworks way too fuckin' close," I said between my clenched teeth. My jaw ticked at the thought of the stupidity.

"Someone's few seconds of a light show cost me my home. I have nowhere to go." Her voice cracked as she shook her head slowly, letting another round of tears fall from her eyes.

"You can stay with me."

The words had a mind of its own, spilling out before I realized what

I had offered. It was an offer I had no plans to take back. I meant it.

Her brows dipped and then rose.

"I-I couldn't do that. I don't even know how long I would be without—"

"I have the space—an extra bedroom and bathroom, all of that. And time… that's not a factor. I just want you somewhere safe until you figure out what to do next."

She sat there, her mouth partially open. Her eyes searched mine for something unspoken. I kept my gaze steady and sure on hers. She pushed out a short breath before saying, "I guess. At least for tonight."

Seventeen

Nina

I wanted nothing more than a shower. In the middle of a vitals check and settling into the reality that my life was only a flick of a flame from being taken, I hadn't noticed how sticky and clammy my skin was or how much smoke was living in my hair. I wasn't cognizant of it until I sat my moistened bottom on the leather seat of Denzel's truck, and my body odor contrasted the spiced tobacco-scented air freshener. When the ignition cranked and the air conditioning blasted through the vents, I quickly adjusted them so that they aimed upwards, not at me. I answered Denzel's concerned eyes with a not-so-much of a lie that I was a little chilly. The option of having the windows down during our 15-minute drive from Fire Company 143 to the suburban neighborhood he lived in was more comforting for my insecurity about my body odor.

I recognized Denzel's community as one of the newer developments of Lovey's Bay, Shore Crest Landing. It was only a few years old, and I remembered reading that the community's highlight was the quiet shoreline of Lovey's Bay lining the crescent-shaped suburbia of family homes. Shore Crest Landing was on a more serene side of Lovey's Bay, just outside of the gated community of The Coves, the neighborhood that housed million-dollar family and vacation homes. I took in all that I could in the darkness of the midnight hour as we cruised through the community's main road before we turned left onto what I assumed was the road leading to Denzel's home.

Denzel pulled into the driveway of a modern white stucco house with gray detailing and shutters. A soft yellow light illuminated the gray garage before us. He pressed a button on the dashboard's left side, and the garage door slowly lifted to the darkened space. Sensing the truck's entry, the garage's interior lights automatically came on, revealing a mostly bare garage except for a few lawn care items and hardware tools. My eyes zeroed in on three boxes as we rolled to a stop. They were stacked at the stairs leading to a door of the home. I could make out the writing on the side of one box to read, "Shoes." The handwriting had a curve that gave off a feminine appeal, filling my curiosity. Denzel's broad body stepped in front of my window, bringing me away from my thoughts as he opened the passenger door and helped me out. My curiosity peaked again as I glanced over my shoulder at the boxes as we ascended the steps and into his home.

"Welcome to my humble abode," Denzel introduced after flicking the light switch. He lifted his hand and quickly moved it from one side to the other like he was Kiki Shephard displaying the finalists of Amateur Night at the Apollo.

We were standing in a white and marble, pristinely clean kitchen that doubled the size of the kitchen I once had. It made sense now why he was a good cook. The kitchen was tricked out with a state-of-the-art gas stove, a stainless steel refrigerator, and a sizeable chef-style island counter in which hanging pots and pans were installed above it. The amenities in this kitchen were not those of a person who just dabbled in the kitchen. It was a kitchen designed for a chef or someone who enjoyed cooking for their family.

My perception deepened as my sight expanded to the living room area outside the kitchen's perimeter. There was no light in that space; only the kitchen light faintly illuminated the expansive room. I took note of a fireplace to the left, but only quickly, as my eyes grew big at the ceiling-to-floor windows that gave me a darkened glimpse of private access to the shoreline guarded by feathery pampas grass.

Denzel guided me through the living room, a short distance to a door in the left corner. Upon opening, a large guest bedroom and en suite bathroom were revealed. It was decorated in neutral colors, white and tan, in a way that gave a woman's touch.

"The guest room is yours," Denzel said after he gave me a short tour of the space. "For however long you need it."

I scanned the room once more, taking in the gratitude filling my body. If it weren't for him, I would probably be laid up in a hotel room, sulking in my loss. Although that would've been a blessing, I felt even more blessed to have someone—whom I've been carrying through the wringer—think enough of me to extend their home to me. I parted my lips into a soft smile and said, "Thank you, Denzel. For everything…"

I wrapped my arms around his neck, succumbing to the wave of feelings running through me. My body vibrated as he wrapped his arms around my waist, heightening those emotions and others from tonight's events. I was shocked by the fear that still sat in my muscle memory of being trapped on my balcony. Then, there was the relief of being rescued from it all. But the feeling that stood more significant than them all was the intense adoration I held for Denzel for choosing to save me. He could've easily let another one of the firefighters do the job, but he did it. He encouraged me to remember who I was. Although it is his job to perform the act of saving people from fiery situations, it felt different that he risked his life for me.

"Why?" The question that was meandering my thoughts came from

Smoke Signals

my mouth. I pulled back, searching his eyes through my misty pupils. "Why'd you come for me?"

His eyebrows dipped low as he answered, "Why wouldn't I?"

I shook my head, refusing his answer.

"No, seriously, Denzel. Why? I've been avoiding you for weeks. I know you have to do this—"

"Because you're worth the climb," he said slowly, emphasizing each word. His irises burned through me, melting away the thin layer and keeping my tears intact. Those words etched the image of his last text to me in my memory.

His cheek ticked, revealing a half smile as he murmured, "I texted you those words, and I meant it. Whatever this wall you have between you and me, I am willing to climb it for you. I'm willing to climb it and help you break it down so that you can see that I am not spitting game. I genuinely want you. So, to answer your question of why...why wouldn't I? If I'd climb walls, I'd climb a burning building for you."

Time stood still as we stared into the depths of each other's souls. Our magnetism pulled, causing us to bob our heads toward each other. We dipped our faces so close that our lips ever so softly grazed, but I would not allow myself to fall entirely into the electrifying pull. That was until Denzel pressed me further into him and pulled my bottom lip into his mouth, sending all my reservations fleeing. I moaned softly as my lip plopped from between his, that being enough for him to swipe his tongue into my mouth, further unraveling me.

Our kisses grew intense and passionate, with Denzel cupping the back of my head as he attempted to devour my mouth. I loved it, feeling enamored by Denzel as he gently tugged at my curls in his hand and exposed my neck, trailing kisses down the side. For once in the last two weeks, I was not fighting myself. I didn't want to fight it. I needed it....but I needed that shower more.

I slid my hand between us and gently pressed against his chest, pulling away from his embrace. He looked at me confused, his look softening when a half smile crept on my face.

"I...really need a shower," I reluctantly said.

He nods and steps back, putting his hands in his pocket. His cheeks turned red as he looked down and back up at me. A dimple activated on his cheek as he said, "Right. It's been a long day for both of us. Let me go grab you a T-shirt or something."

I thanked him before he left me to tend to my hygiene needs. I quickly shuffled to the bathroom and began a steamy shower. Peeling off my sodden dress and panties felt like shedding dead skin. With each layer, I felt free of the weight from the day, and as I stepped under the pressure of the rainfall showerhead, I exhaled a hearty sigh, thankful for the moment and for seeing the end of the day without any bruises.

I jumped at the sting to the outer part of my thigh. I saw the soap suds running over a gash I was unaware of. It was a thin slither that I could only assume happened in my haste on the balcony, perhaps coming from my wine glass. I carefully rinsed it off and then used the same care as I dried myself. Wrapping a towel around my breasts, I took a hand towel and dampened it with warm water. I returned to the room with the rag and some lotion I found and sat on the edge of the bed, patting the wound clean. A few raps came from the outside of the bedroom door.

"You can come in," I answered, still focused on my leg.

"Sorry, it took me a minute. I jumped in the shower, but here's a Tee and some shorts...you good?"

I looked up to find Denzel already treading toward me, his eyes on the wound I was nursing. Jumping into medical mode, he kneeled on one knee and examined my exposed thigh.

"It must've happened while I was on the balcony. I had a glass of wine and probably broke the glass," I explained. Denzel took the rag from my hand and gently wiped at the thin layer of blood that was still seeping from the cut.

"Sit tight," Denzel ordered, getting up and leaving the room.

After a few moments, he returned with an ointment and bandages of various sizes. He knelt before me again, motioning for me to lift my leg, which he extended over his bent knee. My thick thigh was now uncovered and at his disposal, as he squeezed the ointment onto my wound and gently rubbed it in. The simple feeling of his strong hands on my thigh made my love below quiver, and I squeezed my inner thighs slightly. He must've noticed my subtle movement because he peered up at me with a lustful smirk. I slid my teeth across my bottom lip, chuckling at the silent but sexy moment we were having.

Denzel's eyes bounced from mine to the bottle of lotion beside me. "Pass it to me."

I looked at the lotion, and my heart quickened at his order. "What? No, I can put it on. You don't—"

"Pass it to me." The words came out slow and with gentle authority, his mouth still fixed in a soft smirk.

I obliged and passed him the lotion, biting on the inside of my lips as I watched him squeeze a healthy dollop of cream in his veiny hand. He emulsified it between his hands before slowly and firmly smoothed his hands up from my ankle to my calf. My breath slowed as his hands moved up my thigh, stopping just short of my love below before he dragged his hands back down my leg and repeated. I released a shaky breath as his hand trailed down my leg, the pressure of the pad of his fingers causing a euphoric sensation. When he bent my foot back and began to apply gentle pressure just under the ball of my foot, he elicited a breathy moan from me. I popped open my eyes, startling myself, to find Denzel looking at me. His eyes were dark as he licked his lips. He huffed a quiet laugh through his nose before lathering his hand again and working on my other leg and foot.

He continued this for a few more quiet minutes. I fluttered my eyes closed again, relaxed but also feeling myself being aroused by his hands on each leg now, moving up and down in what was now a sensual feeling massage. I silently wished he would touch my love below with each ascend, but he stayed respectful. That alone turned me on. With his last venture up my leg, I fluttered my hooded eyes open and took my hand to his right hand. He peered at me as I guided his hand to my sex. The heat of his hand made me shiver with anticipation. I parted my legs slightly, my eyes speaking my invitation for him to touch me. He understood my invitation and slid his hand up between my slick folds and then scissored my pearl between two fingers.

I arched my back and gasped as he opened and closed his fingers around my pearl, gently tugging as he closed around her, encouraging her to bloom. She did, and I whimpered as the sensation of my arousal began to build. Denzel took his left hand and spread my legs wider, exposing me further. I gasped at the feeling of two thick fingers gliding into me. He stroked my walls, and with each stroke, my juices built and spilled. I bit down on my lip, trying to settle the panting breaths growing in my chest.

And then he stopped. My eyes opened when I felt him slide out of me. His gaze met mine before he moved his attention to his glistening fingers, rubbing them together. Smirkin,g he rumbled, "Beautiful, Goddess."

I wasn't sure if it was a compliment for me or my pussy, but it sent waves through my body. I bit down on my lip hard in agony as I watched him submerge the fingers into his mouth, one by one. He savored my taste like I was a T-Bone Steak.

"Mmm," he moaned his satisfaction, meeting my eyes again.

I was unraveling with each second that passed with his gaze on me. He sat there, not making a move, and I knew he was not making moves because he was waiting for me to give him "the rope." He had every strand of my internal rope, and I wanted to feel special. I wanted to feel him. I removed my leg from his lap and scooted to the edge of the bed. I allowed my legs to fall open with his face now eye level to my love below. He looked up at me in an adorning way that made me cream, and my nerves burst. I placed my hand on his head, running my fingers through his waves. His eyes drifted shut as he bit on his lip.

After a tormenting silence, Denzel slowly opened his eyes to me and whispered, "What do you want?"

"Taste me," I whispered without any hesitation.

A half smile grew on his face, and then I watched him adjust to be on his knees. His heavy dick swung from his basketball shorts, and I gnawed at the inside of my mouth at the sight. He gazed at my love below before hooking my legs into his arms and pulling me so that his nose was grazing my lips. A whimper fell from my lips, desperately wanting to feel his touch. Unhurried, he placed my legs on his shoulders and dived into my love below.

Denzel mouth was magical. He french kissed my love below with languid pecks and licks like he loved her, making me whimper with every tender kiss. He rushed nothing, dragging his tongue between my folds and around my pearl to finally enclose his lips around her, sucking firmly and pulling her out even more. My whimpers turned labored when he pulsed his tongue against her like a heartbeat. I fell back onto my elbows, totally submerged in the pleasure of his act as he started to stroke his tongue up and down like it was a bow and I was his violin. He strung my chords like he was playing the last chords of a Beethoven piece. He sunk his tongue inside my walls as he pulled me into him even further, hooking his arms under my legs and clasping his hands together, locking me in for his final solo. This time, he strummed my pearl with his tongue like he was Jimmi Hendrix with quick, riveting flicks that had me singing along until I couldn't anymore. The rope that was once my guarded heart unraveled with my orgasm.

Eighteen

Denzel

If it weren't for the night Nina and I crossed the line, you would've thought we were roommates with no chemistry. We've been passing each other like the sun and the moon for the last week. As much as I wanted to stay and watch over Nina, I was Chief, and I had to return to the station and work a week's worth of overnight shifts. When I was leaving for work, she was heading to bed. This week, time was not of the essence for us to spend time together. May that wasn't such a bad thing, with Nina having a lot of daunting things to take care of with her apartment.

When I got up from sleeping my Friday away after my long week, I thought it would be a good time to catch up with Nina. So, when I reached the bottom of the steps and didn't find her in the kitchen, and the light was off in her room, my heart dropped with disappointment. I padded into the sun-kissed living room and peered out to the beach, where I found her. She was sitting on the beach in a way that looked like her knees were tucked into her chest with her arms around them, facing the water. I decided to walk out and join her.

"Fire Goddess," I greeted her playfully as I approached her. She jumped and whipped her head in my direction. I winced, realizing I startled her. "My bad, I didn't mean to scare you."

"It's okay," she breathed as she chuckled off her nerves. "I was just in my thoughts. I didn't even hear you walking up."

"The waves will pull you in every time," I said, sitting on the lukewarm sand beside her. "What's on your mind?"

She relaxed her arms from around her knees and stretched them out a bit, burying her feet in the sand. She glanced at me with a smile that didn't quite light up her face and then returned her gaze to the rushing water.

She sighed and admitted, "Everything. My apartment. Where I'm going to go. They said the fire caused a lot of damage in my living room, enough for them to condemn me for not going there alone."

I blew out a breath and nodded. "I agree with them. You don't know what else could be dangerous there—live wires, for example. I'm sure the air is still smoggy in there, too. And the structures…you just gotta be careful. I'll go with you when you're ready. I'm Chief and someone they'd approve of going in with you."

Her smile ticked a little brighter but still didn't reach her eyes. "Thanks. I do need to get in there and grab some clothes. I don't want to spend any more money on clothes. After this, I will need all of my coins to get my life back on track."

I put my hand on her shoulder and gave it a light squeeze, prompting her to shift her eyes to me. I chuckled and said, "Nina, there's no rush. I told you. Stay here as long as you need. This shit isn't a fix that happens overnight."

She sighed as she took in my words and leaned in, placing her head on my shoulder. I wrapped my arm around her, reassuringly squeezing her, and turned my head into her, letting her curly top tickle my chin. Having Nina in my arms felt like peace.

"I just don't want to overdo my stay," she said after we had set in our silence for a beat.

"You can't overdo your stay. I enjoy you being here, even though I haven't really seen you all week."

"Yeah, we haven't seen each other much this week," she agreed. I had the house to myself to snoop."

I bunched my eyebrows together.

"I'm just playing," she admitted, looking up at me and giggling.

"You can snoop," I shot back, keeping a straight face. "There's nothing to hide but my sweaty draws."

She threw her head back, breaking into her snorting laugh that sends me over whenever I hear it. Like clockwork, she snorted and wheezed and snorted again. She clasped her hand to her mouth, trying to stop her snorting fit.

"Who would've thought a sound like that would come from a tiny person like you?" I asked, chuckling at the scene. "If I didn't know any better, I would've thought you had a Volkswagen horn in your nose."

"Ha!" She burst out into another snorting fit. At this point, we sounded like an odd pair of cackling hyenas. Nina shoved me in my chest and mustered out, "This is all your fault!"

My brows reached for my hairline as I snickered, "Blaming me for your malfunctioning laugh is wild work."

Nina tightened her lips around the smile I was happy to see and crossed her arms. Her defiance was cute and pulled at my heartstrings. I pulled her into me again and kissed her forehead. At the press of my lips, her shoulders untensed as she placed a hand on my chest, sinking into my embrace.

"All jokes aside," I said after we settled. "You can go into any room you want in this house. You won't find any skeletons behind any door."

"Hmph," she huffed. I ticked my head down at her, wondering what was behind that huff. She wore a smirk as she lifted her eyes to me.

"Yeah, because your skeletons are in plain view."

"What?" I chuckled through my question.

"Those boxes in the garage."

I opened my mouth to question her but paused when it came to me. Thandie's boxes were in the garage. I slowly closed my mouth.

She giggled. "Mmmhmm, *those* skeletons."

"It's not what—"

"...what I think?" She finished my statement for me. "I *think* it's some of your ex's stuff."

I was stuck catching flies again. "Okay, maybe it is what you think, but it's not."

Nina let out a short laugh. She sat up and looked at me with an eyebrow raised and arms folded again. "What does that even mean, Denzel?"

I dropped my head and quietly groaned at the mess I made with my words and to have to talk about Thandie.

"It means it is some of Thandie's stuff, but it's nothing serious...just a couple of boxes she hadn't picked up yet."

Nina sat silently, her mouth moving as if she was biting the inside of her mouth, leaving me to wonder what was going on in her head. She finally said, "They say that when someone holds on to a memory or *things*, they aren't over whatever it reminds them of."

"I'm over Thandie," I confessed without hesitation. When I'm done, I'm done. But when I'm not, I profess I'm climbing walls or burning buildings for what I'm not ready to give up on."

Nina's eyes softened as her mouth twitched at her fight not to smile. Her smile lost that battle as her gaze drifted down to her hands.

"I really gave you a hard time," she confessed. "Ghosting is usually not my thing. I'm the one that's usually getting ghosted."

"So I come around, and you turn into Casper the Ghost?" I smirked at her, keeping the banter light.

"You got jokes tonight, eh?" she snickered before becoming serious again. "I was scared of losing myself way too fast. I had done that before and didn't want to do it again. I missed all the signs the last time because I was in La La land."

"Fair," I said, taking in her perspective.

"Not really," she corrected. "When I was up on the balcony, getting ready to be swallowed by that fire, I started thinking. I legit was about to die by myself when I didn't want to be by myself. That's when I realized, instead of losing myself in the present, I lost myself in my fears."

I nodded my head slowly, taking in her subliminal confession. She *had* been thinking about me the whole time. This revelation comforted me because I felt similarly like I had let my soft-ass heart lead the way into another situation that was leaving me high and dry.

After another beat, I let my ego do the talking.

"You weren't going to die. Especially not on my watch."

She scoffed. "You're so sure, huh."

"I am," I said confidently. "I'm sure about that…and I'm sure about you."

She licked her lips as her smile grew and then heaved heavily.

"Well, I know what I'm sure about right now," she purred, raising an eyebrow.

I raised an eyebrow back. "What's that?"

Her eyes lit up.

"I'm sure we need to find something good to eat pronto."

She dropped her head into my chest, giggling at herself. I snickered and wrapped my arms around her. I tickled her sides without warning and said, "C'mon, V-Wagon. Rev up your engine so we can go find something to eat."

Nina shrieked and squirmed as she broke into her infamous laugh, pulling me into the sand.

Nineteen

Nina

"I mean, honestly, you can't really compare the two. They are two completely different rappers," I argued, hopping onto the island counter and taking one of the two spoons from Denzel's hand. "Kendrick is a "rapper" rapper. Drake, he's a lover boy rapper."

Denzel chuckled. "What the hell is a "rapper" rapper?"

Giggling, I explained, "You know, someone who is a lyricist, who can really spit."

"Drake has some bars, too."

"Yeaah, but he has lyrics for the ladies, not for battling. I don't even know why he crossed over and tried to act all hard."

"Probably because people say things like he's a lover boy rapper. You basically called the man soft!" Denzel cracked up, his laughter echoing through the kitchen.

I snickered, kicking my feet. "I did not call him soft. I said he was a lover boy."

"Same thing."

"What are you now, Team Drake?"

"I'm Team Denzel all day," he said, lifting his head with a smirk.

I pursed my lips and eyed the small single-serve peach cobbler in his hand. He had begun scooping his spoon into the side of it as if we weren't supposed to be splitting. "Mmmhmm, how about you, Team Bring-That-Peach-Cobbler-Over-Here?"

Denzel jerked his head back. "Damn, if you're hungry, just say that."

I sucked my teeth and dipped my spoon into the nearest corner of the cobbler as Denzel drew near. "Nah, you say that. How are you going to get a scoop before I do?"

"My bad, my bad, greedy." I dropped my jaw, and he released a crooked smile and backtracked. "You know I'm playing."

I rolled my eyes playfully at him before cramming the small mound of syrupy peaches, bread, and cinnamon sugar into my mouth. I paused, and my eyes drifted closed as I let out a slow, endearing moan.

"Oh my gawwd," I dragged, letting the decadent dessert tumble around in my mouth as I chewed. I opened my eyes to Denzel, who looked at me with a smirk as he finished his bite. "Who did we order from again?"

"Baby Dee's Barbecue. It's good, right?"

"Mm-hmm," I hummed while savoring the last sweetness. Without hesitation, I went for another scoop; this piece was slightly bigger than the previous one. I devoured the spoonful, throwing my head back in another exaggerative moan.

"Shit, I'm a little jealous of this cobbler."

I raised my head, squinting my eyes at Denzel, catching his drift. His mouth was now curved into a sexy grin as his eyes went from mine to my lips. My insides flushed, and I licked my bottom lip, tasting the sweet residue from my dessert, secretly imagining other sexy ways to have dessert.

"You missed a spot," he said, diverting his brooding eyes to mine.

I frowned slightly, getting ready to swipe at my mouth, but caught my hand and replaced it with his warm tongue pressed against the lining of my bottom lip before he enclosed his lips into a sensual kiss. He tugged at my lip before hovering in my airspace, sending ripples through my body. My eyes narrowed at him as my mind ran wild at how sexy his clean-up of the cobbler drippings was. Now, my kitty was dripping as I was lusting for him to clean her up.

"I couldn't help myself," Denzel whispered into my lips. "You looked too good to pass up."

I huffed out a quiet laugh, licking my lip again. He chased after my lip with a flick of his tongue, snatching my breath and every ounce of my sense besides the inkling of sense that remained and urged me to indulge in what I wanted. And God, did I want Denzel.

This want has haunted me since our last encounter during my first night here. His lips on my pussy lips left an imprint on my brain and a permanent quake in my center anytime I thought about it. After that moment, I knew it would be hard not to want to indulge in anything further. This moment while we nibbled on each other's lips proved it true.

He pecked at my lips. I pecked back. We collided and fell into a leisurely yet sensual kiss, savoring each other's lips in between our tongues dancing. With each bob and twist of our heads, we grappled for domination of each other's mouths until Denzel slid the half-eaten dessert onto the counter and then moved between my legs, pulling me into him. With one hand pressed against the small of my back and the other running up my back and to the back of my neck, Denzel took control of my mouth, swiping his tongue deep before pulling and sucking on my bottom lip again in a way that sucked a whimper from me.

"Just fuck me already," I whispered into his mouth, almost begging. My composure was failing, and lust was winning. I wanted nothing more but for him to finally fuck me in every way I have been imagining since I first met him.

"Say less."

It was the only thing he said before our lips collided with more passion than the moments before. My pulse quickened as his hands roamed under the tank top I wore, cupping my sensitive breast. My mouth fell open with nothing but shaky breaths leaving them as he rolled my pebbling nipple between his thumb and index finger and then plucked it to further submission. I hissed through my teeth as the warmth of his mouth on my right breast was felt, and then I audibly moaned as his tongue flicked and circled my nipple. I slid my arms against the cold counter as I arched my back as he feasted on my breast, feeling like the goddess he was always calling me. Denzel placed his hand on my back again, keeping me close as he showed the other breast and nipple the same love.

My pussy was throbbing for him now, and she jumped with each accidental collision of his hardened erection through his basketball shorts to my thigh and then at my core. After his feast on my breast, he removed my top, the cold air prickling at my painfully hard nipples. I helped him out his T-shirt, taking in his hairless, chiseled chest, mindlessly running my tongue over my top lip.

He quickly took my lips into his mouth again, kissing me fervently. In between kisses, he whispered, "I can't take my lips off of yours."

"You're supposed to be doing something else," I whispered back before kissing him back, sliding my hands down the curve of his hips and over his muscular ass. I moved my hand under the band of his shorts and pulled them down. I sunk my teeth into my bottom lip as his heavy curved dick bounced at its release.

I broke our kiss so that I could admire his long, thick dick. Chocolate like him and intricate veins protruding. The mushroom of the head glistened from his pre-cum, and I was hungry to taste it. Denzel took his eyes from his dick up to mine, where his brooding desire for something else flickered. I gasped as he forcefully pulled me to him by my cotton shorts.

Denzel mumbled, "I got you," before hoisting me up and swiping the shorts down, throwing them somewhere behind him. I was completely naked now, having not worn any panties under my shorts, and my body was shaking from the cool air and anticipation. He stood before me in his glorious nakedness, too, with a look in his eyes I could not comprehend.

"I'm going to fuck you, Nina," Denzel declared in a dominant tone I had never heard him speak in before. I tuned in and was turned on. He spread my legs wide and pressed them back, forcing me to lie back on the cold marble. "But first, you deserve to be worshipped, my Fire Goddess."

Wasting no time, Denzel buried his face into my vibrating pussy, causing my legs to shake at every swipe of his tongue at my sensitive pearl. I went from panting to whimpering as he devoured me like I was the decadent dessert. The way he groaned as he feasted, I knew I was the decadent taste he was hungry for. He graciously lapped at it each time I spilled my juices like I was the Fountain of Youth.

"You taste so good, Goddess," he spoke into my love below. His words made me moan in reverence. I heaved and moaned louder as I felt his fingers glide into me as he suctioned my pearl. He sucked, then commanded, "Cum for me, Goddess." I moaned and felt my nerves tingling. He sucked harder and then commanded, "Rain down on me, beautiful."

"Oh…my God, Denzel," I panted, feeling light-headed and high off his pleasing tongue. I trailed my hand to the back of his head, subliminally requesting him stay there.

"Rain down on me, Goddess," he commanded again and then turned his sucks into quick pecks to my pearl as he thrust his fingers deep into me. He hooked his fingers, pressing a button that had me crying out

Nina

his name, pulling my arousal closer and closer until I began to wail out as my hips bucked into him.

"Yes, Goddess," he groaned as he cleaned every drop of my essence as it spilled.

"Fuck," I practically panted, running my fingers through my curls. Still in my delirium, I looked over my body to Denzel, who was standing, stroking his gorgeous dick. "Can I serve you this dick, Goddess?"

I pouted my lips, meeting his gaze with my lustful one. Playing along, I said, "You may."

He smirked as he helped me sit up. With a hand on my back, he scooted me to the edge of the counter again, his dick simultaneously entering me but only filling me halfway. I tensed. In response, Denzel kissed me in the most tender way as he slowly rocked into me. The kiss was slow, sweet, and caring, making me feel safe to be free with him. My walls stretched and opened for him, and he began to fill me with each rock. When he was completely in me, he stroked my walls like I've never had them stroked, with long strokes that had my toes curling. I wrapped my arms around his broad shoulders and kissed him deep as his strokes became shorter and harder, eliciting him to lift me from the counter. With his hands under my ass, he pounded me deeper and harder, causing me to break our kiss for the sake of moaning out my ecstasy. He was so deep in me that the collision of our thighs created the background music to our grunts and moans. We sounded beautiful.

"You feel...so...good, Goddess.."

"Fuck, Denzel. You're gonna make me cum again..."

Every time he called my Goddess, I found my crown illuminating. I've never felt this regal before, and with every affirmation, Denzel ensured I owned it. I threw my head back, accepting each deposit of royalty his dick was giving me. I wanted more. I needed more.

"Get on the counter with me," I said breathily through a slow stroke.

Denzel looked at me inquisitively but obliged, placing my sweaty bottom back on the counter and hopping on beside me, dick hard and swinging. He looked at me with a smirk, still questioning with his eyes. The counter was long and wide, with enough room to serve a whole meal and for us to have some fun. I looked at him and requested, "Lay back on the counter."

He huffed a quiet laugh and obliged, positioning himself in the middle of the counter and lying back, his head resting by my thigh. He looked up at me, and I looked down at his dick, erect and looking tasty. I climbed on top of him and hovered my pussy over his face, and then took him into my mouth. He grunted at the feeling of my mouth moving up and down his shaft but then didn't waste the opportunity to pull my ass down until my lips were on his lips. We hungrily went to work. I slurped and bobbed and licked. He slurped and lapped and licked. I moaned and swallowed him. He groaned and devoured more of me. I rocked my hips into his tongue while he thrust into my mouth. It was a whirlwind of pleasure circling up my body, wanting to release, but I needed to feel his hardness inside of me again.

I ceased our feast just before my climax and shifted my position so that I was facing him. I widened my hips and mounted his girth, moaning every inch of the way. He felt so good as I took all of his thickness. I rolled my hips slowly until I was stretched and then began to bounce up and down on him at a steady pace. He was groaning now, his jaw clenched as he tried to hold back his climax. He grabbed hold of my hips, guiding my hips to rock on him, and I did. I rode him like I was the first-place holder at the rodeo. He reached down and pressed my clit, activating a new height to my pleasure.

"Oh shit, Denzel," I whimpered, rolling my hips harder.

"Mm-hmm, Goddess," he moaned, thrusting up into me.

I gasped at the sudden arousal from his movement, ticking me closer to my climax. My mouth hung open, heaving with each thrust of his long dick, finding its way deeper inside of me. My climax climbed just as my hands went from pressing onto his chest to up my stomach, over my breast, up my face, through my hair, and then grasping onto an empty hook between the pans that hung above us.

"Ahh...Denzel...I'm going...to cum..." I heaved and cried as his thrusts grew harder and deeper, bouncing me up and causing my arm to collide against the pans, creating a new tune in between the gushy sounds coming from my center and our thighs smacking. I moaned. He grunted. He thrusted...thrusted..thrusted...

"Shit, Denzel....!"

"Yes, Goddess...fuck yessss!"

Twenty

Denzel

I don't know if the night that Nina and I took the "dip into Lake Minnetonka" was a gift or curse. If it was a curse, it was a sweet, delectable curse that I couldn't stop indulging. The gift: it was the night of my eleventh and final work day of the month, and I had two weeks off. Two weeks off from work that turned into two weeks of me and Nina not being able to stay off of each other, entwined with each other. The weeks were hazy with exploration, admiration, and unadulterated sensations.

Fuck, Nina had me stuck in a soft place—literally. One morning, I woke up to her sweet essence and thigh as my pillow. Since I was there, I made her my breakfast. I damn near knew her body and what made it quake and quiver. Like, she loved her nipples licked, sucked, and flicked until they were standing in permanent attention, and when they were there, I shouldn't stop there. I should keep flicking my tongue and twisting her nipples until she unraveled.

And when she unraveled, fuck, it was glorious. Listening to her cum made me bust one time. We lazily lounged on the couch one rainy afternoon, watching something random. We went from watching something random to her randomly ass up and my face deep into her slick, bald pussy. Her slow moans mixed with her angelic whimpers had me rocked up, dick throbbing, but I was in a trance of her idyllic sounds. I remember pressing my dripping tongue into her love and stroking her walls, imagining being balls deep in her, and then she did it. She wailed her release, shooting a lightning-speed rush through my body, and I released a thick ending all over my abdomen. I remember blinking my eyes open wide as I grunted at my hard release. I was embarrassed for busting and not even being in her, but when Nina turned over and pushed me back and cleaned my release up with her tongue, that embarrassment subsided. It was replaced with pleasure as she swallowed my quickly bricked dick.

Nina….she was fucking insatiable. I was drowning in the literal and figurative essence of her, and I didn't want to be saved.

Twenty-One

Denzel

"Daamnn, I didn't know those patches could grow in!" Deacon boomed loud enough that his voice collided with the 50 Cent song from the gym speaker. Catching me off guard, his sweaty palm connected to the side of my face, landing on the 2-week shadow of a beard that had grown out while I was off.

I swung my arm back, my forearm smacking the drenched undershirt covering Deacon's chest just before he jumped back and cackled. I cringed, partly from the feeling of Deacon's sweat on me and partly for his audacity to try to son me in front of his usual victim, Tevin.

"Yo Deac, I ain't yo' bitch," I said, wiping the back of my arm on my shorts and stretching my jaw. I pointed at Tevin, who was intently studying himself doing arm curls in the mirror. "Tevin's right there!"

Hearing his name, Tevin paused mid-curl, then dropped his arms and shoulders. He tilted his head and looked at me with shock and a hint of disappointment as he asked, "Now how I get in it?"

Deacon and I roared before we said in unison, "Collateral damage," and then howled out again.

Tevin dropped his weights and snatched up his water bottle from the ground. Squirting a water line into his mouth, he stepped over the weights, fussing, "Ya'll stay on my neck. One day, I'm going to—"

"Youngblood, you ain't gonna do nothing but sit yo' ass down!" Deacon cut in, cackling.

"Aight, man," Tevin muttered.

I patted Tevin on the back and copped a squat on the bench beside him.

"You know it's all love, but we gonna keep coming for yo' ass until you rank up, Little Tevin."

"Shiitt, I'm gonna keep coming for yo' ass regardless," Deacon said, snickering. Tevin muttered something inaudible as Deacon turned his attention back to me. "But back to you. You ain't NEVA been able to grow a beard without patches. Them holes are filled!"

I sucked my teeth. "Man, my beard connects all the time. I just never have time to grow it out."

Deacon smirked, propping his arm on the pullover machine. "It's been two weeks…the same amount of time as any other off time, my dude. Looks like you've been getting some "special juices."

"Juices? What kind of juices?" Tevin asked, fully tuned into the conversation now.

I knew exactly what Deacon was implying, but I wasn't about to give him the details he was hunting for—that I've been factually eating and sleeping in Nina's natural beard growth essence. On the other hand, Tevin looked between me and Deacon, completely oblivious to the innuendo. Deacon and I exchanged glances before bursting into laughter at Tevin's expense again.

"Tev, man, you're never going to get Deacon out of your hair," I said, shaking my head. Tevin looked even more confused.

"Facts!" Deacon barked, snickering. "You a little too wet behind the ears for this conversation, my boy. Just sit in silence."

Smoke Signals

Tevin sucked his teeth and threw his hand. "Man, whatever, "Old Man Deacon." I know you're talking about that "wet wet." I just didn't know Superstar over here was getting some." With a smirk, Tevin twisted his head to me and inquired, "Nina letting you hit that?"

Hit it. Lick it. Slurp It.

I shook my head. "Man, y'all get out of my bedroom."

"Aww, shit! She did!" Tevin squealed, standing up with his hand open for me to dap. I left him hanging. Tevin's face dropped before he sucked his teeth and walked away. "Man, I'm out. Y'all old heads play too much. My Bonita Applebum is waiting for me *anyway*."

We laughed Tevin out of the station's gym before Deacon swiped his towel over the space that he had occupied and sat down. "So, Nina's still at the house, eh?"

"Yeah, she's still there. You saw her apartment. It's cooked, and you know that insurance stuff takes a minute to get right."

Deacon chuckled. "You ain't gotta overexplain like that's why she's still there. You know you like having her in your crib."

I did. I really enjoyed having Nina at the house. The more time I spent with her, the more I didn't want to let her go, and not just because being inside her felt like floating through clouds. She was funny with all her quirkiness and goofy laughs. She was attentive, picking up around the house and washing dishes. Even though I told her she didn't have to do those things, she did them anyway, like it was her house, too. I was getting used to falling asleep with her snuggled under my arms and waking up to her on the opposite side of the bed, or even better, her round ass up against my morning wood. I was comfortable with her, just how we were, and I wasn't sure what it would be like when she figured out her living arrangements.

"It's cool," I said, playing down my real feelings.

Deacon scoffed but didn't pry. Instead, he prodded for something else. "Ain't nothing wrong with catching feelings, my guy. God never intended for us to be alone. I take it you got that Thandie stuff handled, right? The key and her extra shit?"

My gleeful smile faltered. "Uhh, yeah...about that.."

Deacon's eyes grew big as he asked, "You got that woman in your house with your ex-woman stuff in there….*and* she still holding the key?!" Deacon's voice got elevated with each revelation. "I know you like playing with fire, but this is bigger than a fire. This a bomb waiting to go off."

I sighed, realizing how fucked up the situation could get with him putting it that way. Even though I had already talked with Nina about Thandie's boxes in the garage, I was still living happily ever after, without a care in the world, while Thandie still had a key to the house and the ability to enter whenever she chose to.

"You're right. I need to close that door real quick," I said, taking my phone out of my pocket.

"Hell yeah, you do! The fuck?! I don't know why you didn't do that a while back."

I opened the text thread with Thandie's name and began typing.

Me: Hey, you still have some boxes at the house…and the key. Hit me so we can make an exchange.

Twenty-Two

Nina

"We'll come back and get the last two boxes," Denzel said, throwing the box of books onto his shoulder. His T-shirt gripped his bulky bicep as it flexed.

I'm surprised I still have a lip the way this man keeps me chewing the inside of my lip. He looked so sexy in contrast to my smut…. I mean soot-painted living room walls. It was no wonder my mind couldn't decipher; I felt pretty smutty from the thoughts running through my head. The never-ending feeling ran through me all the time nowadays.

Sheesh.

"I think we can get these. They're barely full," I said, willing myself out of my thoughts and smiling softly.

"We got men folks here, girl."

Joni's voice entered before she did. Seconds later, Joni switched her way into view, standing in between me and Denzel. She sat hard into her hip and waved me off as she ordered, "Pay her no mind. Y'all can come back and get these boxes. We'll be here."

Denzel chuckled and playfully saluted Joni as he said, "Got it, boss."

Nina

"You always bossin' someone around. I'ma boss you around," Tevin said, entering the room. In passing, he laid an echoing smack to Joni's ass.

Joni yelped, her eyes glowing with shock, then lowering lustfully as her eyes followed him out of the door. She sighed and murmured, "That little boy always startin' some shit."

I scoffed. "Do y'all even ever stop?"

She smirked deviously and said, "Nope," before she shimmied her shoulders, breaking away from whatever nasty thought I knew she was thinking. With a quick shift, she moved on to chastising me.

"I'ma need you to stop lifting a finger when you got that big ol' giant around."

"It's a habit," I said, shrugging and plopping onto one of the two boxes we had left to load.

"Mm-hmm, I know. You've been used to bustas like Pierre. Thank God for deliverance!"

Joni wiggled her fingers in the air and did a faux praise dance, prompting me to snicker at her. I shook my head and breathed, "You're a mess, but you tell no lies. This is definitely different."

This situation was very different. The seasons had changed, but some things had stayed the same. I was still at Denzel's, but not because I was still waiting on my insurance payout. That came through a week ago, but I still hadn't quite figured out if I would lease another apartment at my current location or start completely anew.

Part of me wanted a fresh start, like in a new community. Even if I chose to move to a different apartment, this apartment community held a lot of memories around Pierre that I was ready to let go of. I wanted a new beginning, making space for…whatever this thing is with Denzel.

I didn't know what to call us, figuratively and literally. One thing I couldn't deny was that it felt good. Being with Denzel has felt good.

Ironically, it felt right. I was comfortable with him and how things were, and honestly, neither of us has been in a rush to change anything.

"So, what are you all doing?" Joni asked. I looked up at her, where she was now leaning against the unscathed kitchen island. "Are you moving in with Denzel?"

I frowned, shaking my head quickly.

"No, umm, not officially. I mean, not at all," I stumbled. "I don't know what I'm doing yet. I'm just there...until I figure out what I'm doing next. It's a lot, you know?"

"Mm-hmm," she hums, pursing her lips. " A lot of fuckin'." My jaw dropped, and she rolled her eyes, continuing, "Girl, you can't lie to me. I see it all over you. You are glowing, and you ain't even doing any goofy, clumsy shit no more. It's like he fixed your equilibrium!"

"Damn, tell me how you really feel!" I pushed out an offended laugh through my still-dropped jaw.

Joni's shoulder bounced as she doubled down, "I did. I'm just telling the truth. You are a new Nina, and I like that for you. I don't blame you for not rushing out of that house. Just don't make that house a home without y'all being on the same page. That's where you messed up with Pierre."

My thoughts drifted to the subtle parallel between the two situations. I moved quickly into making life cozy with Pierre without checking in on whether we were going down the same path, similar to the road Denzel and I were on. The difference was that I never had to guess with Denzel about how he felt about me. He showed me in every way possible—we just never clarified what we were doing at that moment. We've just been enjoying each other, and honestly, I'm not sure if I want to clear the smoky haze yet to find out exactly what we are doing.

"You're right," I said, choosing not to divulge my thoughts.

The front door creaked open, and Denzel, followed by Tevin, crossed the threshold. He walked towards me, extending his hand and helping me up. When I stood, I was face to face with his chest, forcing me to roam my eyes up to meet his peaceful gaze. I swooned, which solidified that I wasn't ready to leave our haze for conversations about our reality.

"You ready to go home?" he asked, his tenor reverberating through my bones.

Home.

I guess it was my home for now. I quirked my lips into a half smile and answered, "Yeah," before he leaned in and kissed me.

Twenty-Three

Denzel

Nina: I have a surprise for you. Come straight here. ☺

Denzel: On my way. 👀

Like an obedient puppy, I placed my phone in the console and pulled my truck out of park, heading directly to my place. I didn't know what the surprise could be. It didn't even matter to me. Coming home to Nina has been the best part of my days lately. Considering this was my last full day off, I had no plans to lollygag after workouts with the crew. I wanted to spend as much time with Nina as possible before I was back on a 24-hour shift again.

So, I drove the streets of Lovey's Bay, five miles per hour over the city speed limit, and bopped my head to that popular song by Anderson .Paak and Bruno Mars. The song had a real old-school vibe and resonated with how I felt as I rushed home to Nina.

"I'ma leave my door ooooopen, girlllll…!" I crooned, thankful the windows were closed.

I was ready to hit another high note when a chime from my phone interrupted the song. Glancing at the CarPlay screen, Thandie's name popped up with a message.

Thandie: Cool.

I frowned at the one message text, trying to figure out what she meant by it. It dawned on me that the last message I sent to her was about her picking up her boxes and returning the key. I shrugged and ignored the message, returning to my jam session for the remainder of the drive.

When I opened the garage door and entered the kitchen, the room was filled with an aromatic scent of food and a picture of Nina from the back at the stove, wearing one of my work T-shirts. The shirt was oversized on her petite frame, falling right under the cuff of her cheeks. Although she had plenty of clothes here now, my shirts had become part of her wardrobe at home. Toni! Tony! Tone!'s "Me and You" flowed from the speaker system, filling the room and making it easy for me to tip-toe from the door to her.

I slid up against her, wrapping my arms around her waist. She jumped slightly at my presence but then peered over her shoulders with a welcoming smile. I rocked her from side to side to the beat of the song, and she leaned back against me, exposing her neck just enough for me to bend down and nuzzle into it before nibbling on her ear.

"How was your workout?" she exhaled, drifting her closed eyes open. She placed the wooden spoon she was holding on the side of the stove and put her hands on top of mine.

"Good," I murmured into her ear. "I'm ready for another one, though."

I pressed against more, letting my hardened state be known. She snaked around to face me and placed her hand against my chest. Giggling, she said, "No, because I made dinner tonight...by myself...and I didn't burn anything!"

I raised my eyebrows and chuckled, peering over her shoulder at the encrusted salmon on the stove. "Look at you, babe. Can't call you Fire Goddess anymore."

"We can keep that nickname," she assured with another giggle.

I pecked her forehead before she turned around giddily. She plated the salmon with a side of broccoli and mini potatoes before turning back to me. She shoved the plate and fork in my face and said, "Here. Try it."

I took the plate and fork from her and leaned against the island counter behind me, smiling at her. Her face glowed with pride, and her eyes were big with anticipation. I took a stab at the salmon, and a piece crumbled off. It looked a little dry but edible. I popped the slightly bigger than bite-size piece into my mouth and chewed…and chewed…and chewed the definitely overcooked and underseasoned fish.

"How long did you cook it for, baby?" I mumbled, still rolling the now mush around in my mouth.

Her forehead creased as her breath hitched. "I-I, cooked for—I messed up, didn't I?"

Her smile dropped into a defeated pout, sending my heart spiraling down. I forced the mush down my throat and slid the plate onto the counter, pulling her into my arms.

"It's okay, baby, you tried," I consoled, chuckling as she whined and crossed her arms into my chest.

"It's not okay," she whined. "I really wanted to do something nice. Something different. How do I mess up fish?!"

"It's the thought that counts, baby. Thank you." I chuckled a little harder, squeezing her. Wanting to make her feel better, I scooped her up, causing her to yelp. She wrapped her legs around me for support as I spun her around and placed her on top of the counter. I mumbled into her mouth, "I only have an appetite for one thing right now anyway."

Nina opened her mouth to say something, and I stole the moment to swipe my tongue into her mouth, kissing her deeply. She moaned before returning my intensity, thrusting her tongue against mine. My hands had a mind of its own, runny up her thighs and under the shirt, gripping at the sides of her ass. I was ready to lay her back and enjoy the feast I really wanted when I heard the garage door open. I peered over Nina, who was perched on her elbows before she strained her neck around, both of us meeting Thandie's gaze.

Thandie's eyebrows piqued and then dropped with an expression I couldn't make out. My heart hit the pit of my stomach, realizing the fate Deacon had warned me about was coming to fruition. I moved from between Nina's legs and around the island.

"Thandie, what are you doing in here?"

"I have a key," she reminded, dangling the gold key and folding her arms.

I could hear Nina gasp behind me, and I squeezed my eyes shut, silently cursing myself. I opened my eyes to see Thandie cutting her eye at Nina and then to me. I didn't understand her expressions, but the tension in the room was thick. I turned to Nina, who was now standing, face balled up and smoothing the T-shirt that covered her.

"Nina, give me a second, okay? I'll be right back," I rushed out, my eyes filled with apologies I hoped she would receive.

She sucked in a gasping breath, eyebrows bunched as she questioned, "Are you serious?"

"Just one second," I pleaded, emphasizing with one finger. Nina closed her mouth, but her eyes still showed a mix of disappointment and anger.

Choosing to handle the issue that was Thandie, I motioned for her to follow me out of the house through the garage door. When we were both at the bottom of the garage stairs, I pointed at the boxes still at the foot and said, "Everything you needed to pick up is right here. There was no reason for you to come into the house unannounced."

"I didn't think I had to announce myself. I've always had a key and used it," Thandie scoffed, jerking her head back, her bob bouncing with the movement of her head.

"When we were together," I said curtly.

"Whatever." She rolled her eyes, fluttering her wispy lashes quickly.

I blew out a breath, getting more frustrated at how damning this moment was becoming by the second. I looked at her and scolded, "You were supposed to *call* so we could arrange a time for you to come."

"I text you."

"That's not a call, Thandie," I said through clenched teeth. I inhaled, trying to push away my irritation. "And you said "Cool." I'm no English Teacher, but that's not a question like, "When can I come get my stuff?"

She folded her arms and mumbled, "I didn't think you'd have another woman here."

"Well, I do."

"Who is she?" she dared to ask with her mouth twisted. I frowned at her question. She continued, "I should've known the reason you were telling me to get my stuff and drop the key off was because you had some woman frolicking—"

I put my hand up.

"Pause. I told you to get your stuff because you needed to. It's been six months since we broke up."

"That's enough time to move on?"

I forced out a dry laugh.

"Thandie, don't act like you didn't check out of our relationship six months before we ended things."

Thandie opened and then closed her mouth, trying to find her words. I curved my lip up, folding my arms.

"Right. Listen, Thandie. There's no ill feelings. Nina is a new friend of mine, and I like her. So, I think we need to close our chapter with you taking the rest of your things and returning the key."

Thandie stood there, chewing on her bottom lip, still holding her arms to her chest. In the beat of her silence, I took in her quickly tapping foot, a sign that always clued me in on her irritation or anger. Without notice, she unwound her arms and fidgeted with the collection of keys in her hand. She dangled the single key ring and the golden key. "Here."

The single word came out short and muffled as she barely parted her lips. I ambled closer to her and clutched the key, my finger brushing her palm. With a subtle touch, our eyes met. Her eyes twitched slightly and misted. My eyes narrowed with wonder about this emotion she was carrying and slight empathy for having to have this moment happen like this.

I closed my hand around the key, tucked it into my basketball shorts pocket, and turned, creating distance between us. I held my head low before looking at her and offered, "I'll help you with the boxes."

She shrugged a little, and I grabbed the two boxes, one over the other. I transported them to the trunk of her Audi, which she automatically popped open. When I closed the trunk and turned, she stood there.

Her voice cracked as she confessed, "I didn't think you'd move on—at least not this fast. I guess I took advantage of the good man I once had. I did…I do love you. I just…didn't know if I was ready for what you wanted to offer me. Seeing you…and her…it changes things."

I sighed, stepping back and running my hand down my waves. Her confession would've made a difference if she said it months ago before I unexpectedly met Nina. If she had said this when I was pleading for her to see my vision of creating and raising a family in this home, I probably would've stopped urging and just waited for her to be ready, but what good would that have done? Even though she saw that I was serious about her then, it took her seeing me with someone else.

"Thanks for telling me that," I said slowly, looking everywhere but at her as I tried to find words to say that wouldn't be too hurtful. I settled my eyes to hers, void of emotions. "I'll always have love for you, Thandie. It was good when it was good, but I learned some things about myself when we were apart….and I think where we are now is the best place for us."

Thandie stood mute, her mouth slightly jarred. She blinked once, then twice, before she mustered a solemn smile.

"Oh…Okay. Well, I guess that's that," she said, her voice trailing as her eyes drifted to her feet. She started to walk past me and then stopped, placing her right hand over my left forearm. We looked at each other. "Take care of yourself, Denzel."

My left cheek lifted into a half smile.

"You too."

Twenty-Four

Nina

"Just one second."

Denzel's eyes widen, emphasizing his plea. My eyes ballooned at his request and then darted behind him to the stunningly curvy woman I could only assume was his ex. Calling her by her name would make this moment too real. So, his ex, the owner of the boxes in the garage with the pretty loopy cursive writing on it.

Her handwriting matches her.

It did. The writing was dainty, just like her. She stood with her shoulders back, displaying all of her confidence. She was slim thick, as they would say, thick in all of her womanly glory with a cinched waist that I'm sure was gym-made and not from a bodice hidden underneath the slinky tan cotton mesh dress she wore. It was a dainty dress, provocative but not too revealing, but it was sheer enough that I could tell she definitely didn't have a bodice on underneath. And as she ticked her head in my direction, her voluminous and curly bob swung slightly, falling back in place beautifully. She was bad—like Michael Jackson's bad—and here I was, standing in Denzel's T-shirt and my four-day-old wash-and-go set, looking like Freddie Jackson.

Before I could fix my words, Denzel beelined to the door she entered from, ushering her out. I didn't fully register what happened until the door clicked shut, and I was left alone in the kitchen. When I could decipher my thoughts, the one that screamed out to me was:

She still has a key?!

I scoffed and looked at the digital clock on the microwave, which was glowing at half past eight. I began pacing the floor.

So wait. I've been staying in the house with this man for almost a month, and his ex still has a key? So she just be walking into houses with no announcement? Why does she still have these privileges? Why hasn't he gotten the key back? What the hell am I doing here, doing all of this? I look crazy.

I shook my head at the thoughts scrolling my mind. My face scrunched tighter as I cringed at all the questions I didn't ask and how I ignored the boxes still left in his garage. I legit fell into the lust and coziness of having a man around. That part... just a man. Denzel was not *my* man. We had not solidified anything between us. I've just been letting him slide that heavy dick in me, just letting flags go unnoticed.

"Shiit," I cursed myself through my teeth, throwing my head back in total disappointment at myself. I leveled my head, my eyes zooming into the microwave clock again. 8:46. A sarcastic laugh drew from my mouth as I turned around to do...something. Anything to pull myself from the hole of foolery I was sinking in.

The creak of the door opening halted my movement. I wanted to swivel around in anticipation of answers, but I beckoned myself to take my time turning around to him. I needed time to slow my mind

Nina

before I blurted out obscenities. I turned around and leaned against the counter beside the stove with my arms crossed.

Denzel walked towards me, rubbing his now disheveled waves. He slowly blinked his eyes up to me as he took his position in front of me, leaning against the island counter. We stood silently as a 90s Toni Braxton song played in the background. I was the one to break the silence.

"So, you don't have anything to say?"

Biting down on his lip, he sighed, "I...I don't really know what to say."

I frowned. "Uhh, how about we start by explaining why your ex still has a key to the house?"

He palms his face, his hand sliding down before his shoulder drooped. "Yeah, I...just never got it back."

"So, she can just walk in anytime she wants? What's really going on with you two? Are you still seeing her?"

Denzel frowned and quickly responded, "What? No. I told you, that's been over—"

"But she has a key and boxes here. Yeah, that looks real "over" to me," I rattled off, splaying in some sarcasm. My decision to stay level-headed just flew out of the window.

"I told you about the boxes, Nina."

"But you didn't tell me about the key!" My voice went up an octave, causing my pulse to race.

"Nina, we're not going to do this," Denzel said and shook his head, his tone still leveled.

"It's done already," I quipped, my tone still unchanged. I threw my hands up, falling entirely into my feelings. "I should've known when I saw those boxes. I should've known you were going to make a fool out of me."

Denzel ticked his head, his eyebrows deep in between his eyes. "What? Nina, I never made a fool out of you. I fucked up by not handling this before, but I'm not out to make a fool out of you."

"Yeah, whatever," I dismissed him, moving to walk out of the room. Denzel caught my arm before I could make two steps. I jerked my arm from him and glared. "Get off me."

He threw his hands up, looking shocked but calm in his voice, and said, "Nina, it doesn't have to be all of this."

"You're right," I agreed, throwing my hands. "It doesn't because you are not my man. Hell, for real, I'm just a charity case, a roommate if we want to spice it up—"

"Nina, stop," Denzel said, irritation taking over his words. He took my hand, and when I twitched to pull away, he held on to it firmly, pulling me to him. I hated that his defiance of my temperament melted a piece of the growing ice cap. He took a finger and lifted my chin while I tried to avoid his determined gaze. I failed just as he spoke, "You know damn well you aren't a charity case nor a roommate to me."

"Do I?" I asked, my voice cracking.

He squinted, searching my eyes.

"C'mon, Nina. When have I ever treated you like that?"

I couldn't say anything, partly because looking into his irises made me sink into his sincerity. The other part of me knew he had never treated me like a charity case or like a roommate. Even without the labels, I knew he saw me as more than that. I saw him as more than that. At some point during this month, the lines blurred, and we were moving like a couple. We had been blurring the lines for far longer than a month of our cohabitation. It was different. We were different. I was...

"I'm scared," I admitted, it barely coming out more than a whisper.

"I'm not *him*, Nina," he breathed, peppering my lips with soft kisses.

"I know," I exhaled before pressing my lips to his, totally melting.

"So," he says between another kiss. "Stop treating me like I am him. I know what I want." He kissed me again. "And I want you. I'm still waiting for you to throw me the rope."

The rope of my restraint unraveled as I sunk into his arms, and we deepened our kisses, swiping with hunger. I hungered to be filled with trust in him and his words through each swipe through his mouth. I needed it to fill me so that my fear was no longer. Our connection broke only when he picked me up, his arms cradling my ass as I wrapped my legs around him, and then we were right back at it.

My thoughts weaved in and out of my conscience, swaying from wanting to resist this moment and then to want to fall into my yearning for him. It was far more than just the yearning of my love below wishing to be penetrated by him; it was also my heart. I couldn't get him out of it, and I didn't know when I had let him in. Perhaps it was when he showcased his patience with me with my cooking shenanigans, or more obviously, when he saved me from the fire or was it when he worshipped my body in this very kitchen? I didn't know when, but I was far too gone now.

And here we were, far too gone for me to protest our ascend of the steps to what had turned into not his room but our room. Then, we were far too gone when he laid me across the bed and lifted his shirt off of me, suckling my bare breast and then trailing kisses down my stomach, where he then found home between my legs. I was gone and did not want to turn back when he pulled my orgasm out with his tongue. We were out of this world when he sunk his erection into me, rocking into the deep darkness of my wet space. We were somewhere unknown when we climaxed together.

Twenty-Five

Denzel

I heard Nina tiptoe out of the room, but I didn't open my eyes. I assumed she was going to use the bathroom or something. Instead, I let the night before replay through the darkness of my eyelids, pumping up my morning wood with anticipation of her arrival back to bed. After not hearing a toilet flush, water run, or anything that corroborated my assumption, I opened my eyes and searched the room. The bright rays from the sun beamed through the window, landing on the opened bedroom door, and something hit me in my core. Something like my intuition telling me to get up. So I did, padding out of my room, through the hallway, and down the stairs. As I strolled down, I could hear some shuffling and what sounded like a zipper. I skipped the last few steps and found Nina at the edge of the living room and kitchen...with her suitcase.

She halted, her orbs big and doe-eyed, just like when I first met her, except they didn't possess joy or curiosity. There was a faint tint of red, and they strained with shock and sadness. My forehead crumpled softly as I concluded what her eyes were telling me.

"Nina...what's up? What are you doing?" I forced out in a low, raspy voice.

She sipped in a breath and held it, then chewed on her lip nervously. She tore her gaze from mine and tightened her grip on the handle of her suitcase. Powering towards the garage, she said, "I-I need to go...to think."

"Whoa, whoa, wait, Nina...talk to me," I rushed out.

Her little legs were covered with grey leggings, and she moved fast to the door. My heart thudded against my chest, and I jogged long steps and planted myself before her. I placed my hand on top of the hand holding the suitcase handle and blocked her path. I ducked my head to her eye level, forcing her to look at me. Her chest was heaving, and her eyes were now swelling with tears.

Nina squeezed her eyes shut and pushed out a breath as she slowly said, "Denzel, please move."

"I'm not," I protested, shaking my pulsing head. "I need you to talk to me. Tell me what's going on. Because last night...we were good—"

"Were we, Denzel?" Nina cut in, causing me to pause, mouth still open. "Yes. Last night was amazing, but everything about last night was not good. Your ex, the key...it just brought up a lot for me. I've been so wrapped in following my heart that I stop thinking."

I grabbed her other hand and, almost pleading, asked, "What's wrong with that?"

She pulled her eyes from mine and whispered, "Everything."

"Nothing," I countered, my voice as low as hers. "Because I've been following my heart, too, and it's led me to nothing but good. It led me to you, Nina. Can't you see? When the smoke cleared...literally, you were there. My fire goddess. Nina. Please. Don't run away from this."

If my boys were here, they would probably be clowning me for my plea to Nina. But even then, just like now, I didn't care what I looked like. I didn't want her to run. I didn't want to lose her. I could understand what things looked like with Thandie showing up and her fears. She didn't have to spell it out because I had the same fears. I was afraid. Hell, I was afraid right now. I was afraid of losing her and having my heart left wide open…yet again.

I moved my head, trying to get her attention again. She hesitated before looking at me with eyes that showed feelings between fleeing and staying. I tried again, "This shit is scary for me too, but baby, please…"

She blinked, and a heavy, lone tear fell from her eye.

"I-I can't."

As her voice cracked her answer, so did my heart. She moved from my grasp without effort because my grip had softened at her final words. Then, she left me with my heart exposed.

Twenty-Six

Nina

I left Denzel's home and didn't look back. I ignored the tugging at my heart, urging me to rethink the mistake I was making. I didn't answer his numerous calls or texts in the weeks after. I just left it all behind.

I had been with Pierre for three hopeful years. Two of those years were great. Date nights, great sex, everything felt right and on track to move our relationship into marriage. I wouldn't have been with him for two years if I didn't feel we were moving into something long-term. I wanted the marriage, the family, the white picket-fenced home, so it didn't make sense for me to be with someone I didn't see this happening with. But then, when we got to year three, and I started hinting at wanting to know what our future looked like, Pierre couldn't answer. Well, he answered, but never with clarity, just a bunch of maybes, we'll see, and perhaps. I saw the SOS smoke signals coming from him and just thought that perhaps I just needed to help him along towards a proposal. So I stayed and did everything my mother told me not to do before I got an engagement ring. I took on all the wifely duties, made sure he was fed well, and fucked him good and everything until he just left.

"He wasn't sending smoke signals for me to help him. He was sending smoke signals for help out of our relationship." I said, replaying the memory. I exhaled heavily, letting my words marinate between Joni and me. That didn't last long.

"Okay, girl, I know. I was there!" Joni exclaimed, flicking her wrist up and saying "duh" to me with her ballooned eyes. She huffed and crossed her arms over her chest, sitting back in her space on the couch across from me. "When are you going to stop telling that story? That ain't your life no more!"

I gawked as the truth of her words sucker-punched me. I stumbled over my words to defend myself.

"I mean, it's part of my story. It's why I couldn't continue with Denzel."

"Girrrrl, if you keep letting that dingbat still be a part of your story, you will always end up running from a good thing. Look at you. You're sitting in my little ol' apartment instead of with that human-sized chocolate candy bar because "Pierre left me.."

Joni squeaked her imitation of me, and my jaw was nearly disengaged from my mouth as I defensively said, "I do not sound like that, Joni."

"You do," she quipped. "Girl, you are letting that man run your life, and what is he doing? He about to get married to whole 'otha woman."

I dropped my eyes to my hands, her words being the body hit that TKO-ed my mouth shut. I couldn't argue with her. She was right about everything she so blatantly said.

"You're right," I solemnly admit. "I've been letting the sorry, sad love song that was Pierre and I stop me from experiencing…something good. Denzel was good to me."

"Mm-hmm," she hummed, shaking her head. "He a good man, Savannah." We both giggled at her imitation of the line from Waiting to Exhale before she continued, "That man saved you from being burnt just like your food AND let you stay at his house."

"Why did my cooking have to catch a stray bullet, Joni?" I asked, narrowing my eyes.

Joni waved me off. "Girl, that's beside the point."

Our phones chimed almost simultaneously. I looked down at my phone and gasped at the headline on the screen.

Lovey's Bay Breaking News:
Wildfires continue to plague Robin's Bend Park and County due to the high heat and winds. Residents are ordered to evacuate immediately, and Robin's Bend is reaching out to Lovey's Bay Fire Department for a helping hand. This fire has claimed five lives, one being a fallen firefighter.

"Shit," I muttered, opening the article and reading further. Robin's Bend was only about 30 miles south of us, making Lovey's Bay the closest city to call for help.

Joni's phone chimes again, and she gasps.

"Girl, Tevin said they are heading to Robin's Bend."

I jerked my head up to her. "What?"

She nodded slowly and peered up to me. "Yeah. He said Denzel called him and the whole firehouse crew in."

My stomach pitted as I repeated what I had just read, "A-A firefighter just died out there."

"I know," Joni replied quietly. Abruptly, she jumped up with her phone in hand. "I gotta go call my YoungBoy Big Dick. This might be the last time."

"Don't say that!" I exclaimed, unsure whether to be disturbed by her morbidity or her nickname for Tevin. Joni scurried away toward her room. I stared at the green square that led to my Messages app, my finger hovering over it, contemplating what to do.

I knew what I wanted to do, but I felt like I was too far removed from Denzel at this point. It's been two weeks since I left, and who knows how many calls I ignored before he stopped calling a week ago. I nailed that coffin closed behind my stupid reminiscence of a relationship that wasn't meant to be. Over a man who didn't do half the things Denzel has done for me in a quarter of the time.

Fuck, Nina.

Feeling defeated, I put my phone to sleep and decided to sit on Joni's balcony. I almost decided against it because it was windy tonight in Lovey's Bay. And then there was the fact that the last time I was on a balcony, I nearly died due to high winds, but I went anyway. I needed to face my fears. Besides, there were no fireworks to be whisked in my direction—just a crisp fall chill. I grabbed my cardigan and threw it over my black tube dress before heading out.

Joni's balcony pointed toward the city rather than the beach like mine. Although a different view of our beach town, it was still beautiful to see the cascade of lights across the skyline. It was eerily quiet in Lovey's Bay tonight, though. Even with the subtle hint of fall's approach through cooler nights, September still carried the bustling nightlife of Summer. Tonight was different. Lovey's Bay skyline glowed, but the streets were quiet, with little to no auto traffic. And the street where we lived, usually moderately busy with foot traffic to local nightlife or nighttime joggers, was deserted. I saw maybe one or two people during the several minutes I had been on the balcony.

The blaring of a firetruck siren cuts through the quiet, causing me to jump slightly. My eyes located the fire station a distance away as my gaze settled on the red spinning lights of a fire truck pulling out. I wondered if Denzel was in that truck, and my stomach twisted at the thought of him leaving to risk his life. However, it was not enough to become unstuck from my fear. Well, almost. I sat up in the chair with my feet planted firmly on the cool cement, ready to make a move, but I

Nina

froze. My hands gripped the steel arm handles, keeping me in place.

"Oh, there you are," Joni's voice trailed behind me. I looked over my shoulder, finding Joni at the sliding door. I looked her up and down, noticing she was still dressed in her leggings and shirt for the night but now had on her Crocs and a denim jacket. She cocked her eyebrow at me, noticing my survey of her. "What? I'm going to see my youngin' off. Give him some good luck head or something."

I twisted my mouth in disgust. "TMI."

She shrugged. "Whatever, girl. This might be the last time."

"I wish you would stop saying that."

"Shit, you never know, girl."

I squinted, confused. "I thought y'all were just kickin' it."

She looked around in thought and then brought her eyes to me. She ticked her head and shrugged, saying, "We are."

My face twisted, even more confused about her dedication to Tevin and their status, but I shrugged it off. Another shrieking siren went off, and I snapped my head toward the station again.

"I gotta go," Joni announced quickly. I turned to see her poised to walk, but then she paused and looked over her shoulder at me. "Lil' Tev and I might just be kickin' it, but I know a good thing when I have it, even if it is just dick. You better see your good thing before it's too late. But if you choose to keep your silly ass right here….don't wait up for me!"

Joni switched away, leaving me with an echo of her words.

You better see your good thing before it's too late...

I slumped back into the chair and let out a sound between a sigh and an agonizing groan. The battle between my mind and my heart created this turmoil. It also created the pulsing in my temples and the erratic beat of my heart that accompanied FOMO. The more sirens I heard, the more my nervous system jumped at the idea that I could miss the opportunity to say goodbye to Denzel, not that I thought this would be the last opportunity.

Could it, though? What if this was the last time I had the opportunity to tell him I'm sorry for letting my angst lead me out of the door...that I missed him...and that I was scared at how fast we fell, but even more afraid that if I let another moment go by, I may miss the opportunity to tell him that I care...

I don't know at what point during my teleprompter of thoughts was when I got up and slipped on my thong sandals or when I decided to walk the few blocks to the fire station hastily, but I did. A firetruck whizzing past me pulled me from my trance, and I realized I was a few steps from the station. The yellow light from the garage beamed across the darkened sidewalk out to the street, indicating the garage door was lifted entirely, and then the colliding of voices could be heard bellowing out from within. As I got closer and the voices became more distinct, I paused, realizing I hadn't thoroughly thought this through. I had no idea if he was still there, and here I was, a woman in plain clothes planning to stroll into a fire station amid a crisis.

You better see your good thing before it's too late....

Joni's words haunted my mind. Although the idea of this being the last time to see Denzel seemed a bit of a stretch, I understood her sentiments. I had to decide whether I would self-sabotage my way out of a good thing or get what I wanted and deserved.

Blowing out my jitters, I straightened my shoulders and walked into the garage. The hustle and bustle of the crew packing and loading engines continued, and I went unnoticed as I slowed to a timid pace. That's when I heard a familiar voice.

"Nina?"

I moved my head to the left, where I heard the voice, connecting it to Deacon standing beside an engine being loaded by crew and equipment. My nerves bucked in my body as I searched for words. I opened my mouth but couldn't manage my thoughts into a coherent sentence. Instead, I just said, "Denzel?"

Nina

His brows furrowed and then lifted. "Oh, damn, Nina. I don't think he's still here. He should've left with the crew two trucks ago." Deacon's voice carried a tone of sorrow as if he understood the urgency of seeing him like he knew our backstory.

"Oh. Ok," I said, tears swelling at the lining of my eyes as I accepted his sorrowful words. I sucked in a short breath, pushing back the urge to let a teardrop. I could not break down in this station in front of all these people.

"Cap, we're ready to roll!" A guy in the driver's seat of the truck Deacon stood in front of called out.

Deacon turns his head to him and nods before turning back to me. Regretfully, he says, "I'm sorry, Nina. We're getting ready to roll out. I'll let him know you were looking for him when I see him. Okay?"

I nodded my head, sucking in my bottom lip, still fighting back my tears. I mustered to say okay before he smiled solemnly and hopped into the truck. I took a few steps back as if I was in the way as they pulled out of the garage, leaving me and one lone fire truck in the now pin-drop quiet garage.

After the truck's engine hum and the siren's blare became almost inaudible, I slowly turned to the garage exit. I squeezed my eyes shut tight and blew out a shaky breath accompanied by a heavy, hot tear at the corner of each eye. I shook my head as I scolded myself, thinking about all the gaslighting and avoidance I put in between me and Denzel, only to try to resolve it right before he left for a major wildfire. And who was I to think he would even give me the time or day to right my wrongs after only pushing him away and not communicating what was really going on with me?

"God, I fucked up," I scolded myself under my breath. I swiped at my face to rid my tears and began my walk of defeat.

"Nina?"

Twenty-Seven

Denzel

Something told me to wait on leaving Lovey's Bay. Well, it wasn't a something; it was a call from Robin's Bend requesting more hands on deck for the wildfire. So, I sent the crew I was supposed to be leaving with before me and called Tevin and a few of our crew who were off in for the mandatory travel to Robin's Bend. Things were moving fast, naturally, considering the circumstances, so I hadn't had a chance to let Deacon know I was staying back, but I wasn't concerned. Deacon was my right hand and Captain, so all would be well with him leading while I waited for the last crew.

After hearing the last crew pull out of the garage, I headed toward it to start going through the checklist of things we would need while waiting for the team to come in. I gave them an hour to settle their home affairs before reporting, which gave me some time to settle my mind around what was in front of me. For weeks, my mind had drifted in and out with thoughts of Nina. Thoughts of frustration…disappointment…longing. It was for my betterment that the last couple of weeks didn't consist of life-or-death emergencies because Nina's abrupt departure fucked me up.

They say there are five stages of grief, and I believed I was experiencing them. It started with denial. I didn't think Nina would be gone long. Hell, I didn't think she'd be gone longer than a few hours the day she left. A lot had happened, and I just thought she needed some time to think, like she said. Hell, I didn't blame her. Thandie walking into the house was a lot of me, too, but I thought that considering we talked about my past with Thandie, we would get past it. When she didn't return later that night, I got angry—not angry at Nina, at myself.

I couldn't be angry at anyone but myself. The step to finally closing the door with Thandie was way overdue. I had a conversation with Deacon and me just before the disastrous moment. I slow-rolled, not because I still had hopes and dreams of Thandie and me getting things back on track. That idea was long gone. I just…didn't do it. It wasn't important to me because Nina had become important in my life. I could agree with Nina that things moved and moved fast. What I didn't agree with was that it needed to slow down. Why did it have to if we were enjoying each other?

That's when I started bargaining. Begging was more like it. I called and texted Nina, hoping she would just talk to me. Contextually, I knew she was scared. Shit, she said it, but of what? Of me? Of being hurt again? I could guess that's where the fear stemmed from, but I couldn't be sure because she wasn't talking to me. She just kept running. Kept avoiding. All I ever wanted to do was to answer the call and show her that behind all of the smoke from the demolition of her last relationship, there was me, trying to show her that we ain't all shit.

I sent her one last text a week ago. It was the same message I sent her once before—my final plea.

Denzel: *You're worth the climb. Just throw the rope down to me.*

When that message went without a response, it was like the nail to a coffin. It sealed away the idea that I could sway her to talk to me—to do this. What was this? Shit, I didn't know. It was something I wanted, but I couldn't force a vision I saw on someone who couldn't see it. It was the Thandie situation all over again.

So here I was at acceptance. Had I wholly accepted things? Not quite, but I was past denying it was over. I was past being angry at why it was over. I was done pleading to be heard and seen. And I didn't have time to be sad or depressed. I just accepted what was, and now, I had to clear my mind about it and get focused on what was at hand in the present moment. And that was—

"Nina?"

I knew Nina's petite figure and curly short haircut from anywhere, even with her back towards me, but I honestly thought perhaps this was a mirage. But when she whipped her head around, and her entrancing cinnamon orbs met mine, the feeling that jolted through my body told me this was real. Nina was here. But….why?

My mouth was still ajar, and my face scrunched with confusion as I ambled down the steps further into the garage. She crept towards me until we met just behind the last parked engine. We stood there, me looking down at her and Nina looking up at me with tearful eyes.

"Are you okay?" That was the only question I could think of as I scanned her red eyes.

"I-I thought I missed you. I've missed you.." she stammered, her words trailing off and cracking.

I stood there, still with confusion written all over my face. I didn't know how to take her words. I slowly responded, "I was supposed to be gone, but we got another crew coming in to head out."

She blinked hard as she shook her head, and tears trickled down her cheek. The sight clenched at my heart, but I wasn't sure how to move. I needed her to speak. She wrung her hands and then looked at me with certainty in her eyes. "No, I have *missed* you, Denzel. I thought I missed you and needed to see you before you left...the wildfire...I was worried I wouldn't be able to see you...to tell you...to say...that I missed you...I..."

I stepped to her, and I couldn't resist calming her worried words with a kiss on her soft lips. I could hear her suck in a surprised breath through her nose before she lingered on my lips for a long pause before drifting slightly from our connection.

I caressed away another falling tear with my thumb. Gazing into her dilating pupils, I whispered onto her lips, "I missed you, too."

"I'm sorry," she whispered, moving her head from side to side.

Her lips parted as if she were about to say something else. I pecked her again, stilling her and her words with my own, "I'm sorry." I cupped the side of her face, pecking her lips again, and confessed, "I should've handled things with Thandie a long time ago."

She leaned into me, trailing the light touch of her hand up the side of my face, and kissed me back before whispering, "I'm scared, but I don't want to be scared anymore."

I pulled away just enough to look her into the beautiful irises. They held a fire, and she had no idea she possessed it until I reminded her, "Nina, the Incan goddess of light and fire. You are the light and the fire, Nina. Light that fear up. Let it burn. Then, toss me the rope, Nina. Let's climb to a new beginning together."

A match striking the side of a matchbox. A flick of the ignition of a lighter. A silent detonation of an explosive. That's how suddenly and without notice, the burn between us happened. Our pecks turned into deep, passionate lashes, our tongues intensifying the yearning between us. Two weeks was too long. I missed the feeling of Nina. I missed her lips. I missed her supple skin. I missed her button nose. I adorned a kiss to every part of her face that I missed, pulling out a soft moan from her before I attempted to devour her mouth again.

Smoke Signals

We were stumbling with no direction or destination until her back collided with the rear of the fire engine. That didn't stop us from exploring each other's mouths or the exploration of my hands down the stretchy material of her dress, clawing and bunching the material in my hand as I eased it up her thigh.

"Denzel...your crew.." she moaned as I moved my kisses down her neck, still steadily gathering the material, now pulled up around her bubble butt.

I licked a trail up the side of her neck and then kissed the line of her jaw before kissing her deep before I groaned, "We have time."

I didn't know if we had time. I didn't care. All I cared about was having Nina at that moment before I had to go off and fight a massive fire. Right now, I wanted to immerse myself in the fire that was us. So I did. Dropping down to one knee, I hooked her right leg over my arm and nuzzled my nose up against the lace that housed her fragrant pussy. I pecked against the lace near her opening, her essence dampening my lips through the lace. Like a feral animal, I pounced, pressing my flat tongue against the lace over her button. Nina gasped as I heard the sandal on her raised leg flap to the ground. I took my free hand and moved the lace away, exposing what I wanted. I pulled her clit into my mouth, and I began to french kiss it like I missed her. I *did* miss her.

I could hear Nina's hand sliding against the metal of the fire truck as she desperately clawed to grasp, all while I sucked and slurped and then sucked and flicked. I was ravishing in her dripping feast. I wanted to taste it all. I extended my tongue and probed it into her center, stroking her walls and pulling her essence into my mouth as if her water gave me superpowers. Shit, it gave me a supercharge. I alternated between stroking her walls with my tongue and sucking her pearl, causing Nina's moans to turn into pants, stirring her into a frenzy so much that she grabbed the back of my head to steady on her pearl. So I did. I was sucking and groaning on it, sucking and flicking...sucking and flicking until she unraveled into my mouth.

The fire was still lit. Standing to my feet and my face wet from her essence, Nina pulled me into her, probing her tongue into my mouth. Her kiss was forceful and passionate, and it turned me on, making my dick even harder. I wanted to be in her right now, but she had other plans. Switching positions, she backed me against the fire truck and undid my belt and zipper of my blue slacks. She pulled down my pants and my briefs, my dick plopping out against the coolness of the air before she sunk into a squat and wrapped her warm mouth around my dick. I sucked in a breath and clenched my teeth as she moaned and slurped, working her way down my shaft. Her mouth felt so fucking good. So magical. I rolled my eyes to the back of my head and then looked down at her. She was beautiful like this, entirely in her enjoyment, sucking me off, but I *needed* to be in her.

As hard as it was to pull from her sweet mouth, I did, helping her up and then hoisting her up where she wrapped her legs around my waist. My dick was already familiar and lining up to her center. Turning us around, I pressed her against the truck again and sunk into her, slowly at first, causing us both to let out a satisfied moan. And then I began to rock into her, creating a steady rhythm, inching my way inside her tight walls until she was stretched and my length was completely in her.

The feeling of her depths was hypnotizing on some Voodoo shit. The sound of her juices, her moans, and the slap of our skin was the spell, and I was under it, seeking out to hear it louder, feel her deeper. And when we locked lips again, it was like the sealing of the work. I don't think we were just Nina and Denzel anymore. She was the goddess, and I used my rod to worship her body. I fucked her harder, faster, and deeper. My balls were smacking her ass, and our kiss was being broken by her whimpering moans now. It drove me mad, in a good way. I thrust deeper and then one more time before we both broke into the sounds of our orgasm. We stayed there for a long pause, us both panting heavily between languid kisses as we came down from our explosion until I was soft, and we disconnected.

We cleaned up in just enough time before the crew started filing in. I guided Nina through the garage as the crew meandered through the firehouse. We stood on the sidewalk just outside the garage, wrapped in a lingering embrace. The hug felt different than any other that we had. It felt…permanent. Although it felt permanent, I didn't want to let her go, but I knew duty was calling.

"I don't want to hold you up," Nina said softly, pulling away, leaving only our hands intertwined.

"Yeah, it's almost that time," I say reluctantly.

A beat passed between us before I reached into my pocket for my keys. Locating the gold key I retrieved from Thandie, I unhooked the ring from a larger one and put it in Nina's hand.

"Go home," I requested, closing my hand around her hand.

She looked at the key, her smile timidly unable to stay in place. She started to shake her head and say, "Denzel, I don't want to impose…"

"You're not," I cut in. "I want you there. I want to come home from this crisis, and you be the first person I see."

She huffed a small laugh through her nose as she began to blush. She looked at me and said, "This is so fast, but it feels so right."

"It does," I agreed wholeheartedly. I pulled her into me and kissed her, expecting it to be the last kiss before I left. She pulled on my bottom lip before pulling away, sending a wave through my body. I pecked her lips, this time really being the last, and looked at her with an eyebrow piqued. "See you when I get home?"

Her teeth grazed her bottom lip as a beaming smile overtook her face. "Yeah."

Epilogue

Pierre,

 I wish I could've articulated my feelings to you the day I saw you with your fiancee. Your fiancee. It feels weird writing that when it's not about me. You know, I really saw that outcome for us. You made it easy for me, too. You courted me and said all the right and sweet things that kept me in our relationship for three years. It's crazy because you knew how I felt about long-term relationships. I always said, "My Dad always said a man knows if he wants to be married to you in a year." If he were still living, he would've shook his head at me for being with you for three years and still not knowing whether you wanted to marry me.

 I probably can't blame you completely for being foolish enough to stay. I knew deep down that even though we talked about it, you never were definitive about wanting to marry me. I just held on to hope, hoping that maybe that hope would turn into truth. But this letter isn't for me to dwell on what I could've done differently. This letter is about me releasing you....

 So, Pierre, I'm releasing you and our experience. Our experience served its purpose. We had fun and created some enjoyable memories, but I've learned over the last couple of weeks that the true purpose of us was for me to realize you were in my life to show me that I was playing too small. I was playing myself too small. I settled for mediocrity and half-baked promises when I deserved someone who was sure about me and wasted no time showing me.

So, I release it all and all the feelings that accompany it. I release the feelings of self-doubt. I release the insecurity. I release the fear of being played with again. I release you, Pierre. None of this serves me anymore. You do not serve me anymore.

I exhaled my final release of breath that sat stuck in my throat, watching the black ink dry on the period that closed out my release letter. It held more than just the end of a sentence but an end to a space I could no longer dwell in. I looked up at the tablet I had perched on the marble kitchen island and sat up in the chair, pressing play. Dr. Amerie Dubois' stilled cocoa face and a bright smile began to move, her curly fro moving with the nod of her head.

"Okay, now that you have written out your release letter, here is where the fun begins....the *healing* begins! Take your letter and light it up, Queen! Watch the fire dissolve away all of the pain, all of the hurt, everything that you are releasing in this letter. Let it all burn and feel it leave you. This is your new beginning. Oh, and ensure you do this over a bowl of water, your sink, or the toilet for safe measures."

I scooted the bowl of water I had prepared in front of me, taking the place of the letter and picking up the lighter. I positioned the lighter tip to the edge of the white notebook paper, my finger ready to engage the ignition, but I hesitated. I looked up as if I could watch the scenario playing through my head of me almost burning my kitchen down by accident and then surveyed Denzel's kitchen.

"Nah, we aren't doing that again," I said, shaking my head and dropping the lighter back on the counter. I chuckled at myself and went with a much safer option.

It was early dusk, the point in the day when the sun was on its descent, creating a moody orange in the sky that faded into hues of blue. The contrast was beautiful against the subtle wave of the bay, making it quickly one of my favorite times of day to go outside. I

Epilogue

realized this the first week at Denzel's when I decided to stroll to clear my thoughts about my pending living arrangements. It brought me peace in that stressful time. Taking that same path tonight with the cool sand underneath my feet and the lull of the easy waves of the bay, I felt a similar kind of peace. This peace didn't have the underlying stress behind it. It was peace emphasized by joy.

My feet sunk into the dampened sand as I approached the shoreline. I stopped just as a mini-wave crashed at my feet, sending a chill through my body as the crisp September wind heightened it. Without much more thought, I began ripping the letter into small pieces and finally letting them fall from my open hands. I watched the pieces practically melt as the waves covered and washed them away.

I noticed movement in the house when I reached the deck, and as I grew closer, my pulse raced as I quickened my steps. As soon as I stepped through the threshold and into the living room, Denzel met me, pulling me into his arms before I could close the door entirely.

"You're home!" I gushed as his arms and body swallowed me in our embrace.

"Finally. After two long weeks," he mumbled into my hair. The rumble of his voice vibrated through my body and down to my center.

I looked up to look at him but was met by his warm lips, and I didn't hesitate to invite his tongue into my mouth. I missed him. I missed him so much, and the way his hands glided down my back and palmed my ass all while he hungrily kissed me, I could tell he missed me too. I had so many questions about his time in Robin's Bend, but those questions dissolved just like my letter.

Unlike the letter, my questions sank and dissolved in the waters of my love below as he peeled away the oversized sweater that hung over my body, and I slid down the gray sweats that tented his erection. In no time, we were naked, and my face and hands were pressed against the floor-to-ceiling window, taking every slow stroke he delivered. It was like his speed was intentionally slow to savor every snug thrust into my center. I relished in it too, falling into an oblivious headspace with each plunge, each kiss to my neck or my shoulder, each squeeze of my breast and flick of my nipples. The feeling of Denzel in me was different this time. It always felt good. This time, it felt right and—

"Oh, fuck, so fucking amazing!" I panted just as I opened my eyes to the reflection of his adoring eyes in the window. Just like that, my walls clenched around his dick, and my orgasm unhinged. A whimper fell from my opened mouth as he took his final thrust. His deep groan sent another wave through my body, and his seeds spilled into me.

* * *

"Damn, I didn't think it would take as long as it did. I expected to have the house to myself for maybe a few days."

"Yeah, there are a lot of factors that determine how long it takes us to stop a wildfire: the amount of crew on hand and resources. Our problem was that it started to spread. We needed more crew to contain it."

I was lying against Denzel on the couch. We had just finished a shower and were now lounging, deciding what to eat, considering the appetite we had worked up. When he began to explain why the trip to Robin's Bend turned into two weeks, the imagery of him fighting a massive fire, yet again risking his life, played in my mind, causing me to pause my perusal of dinner options.

I placed my phone down and squeezed the arm that barricaded me to his body, snuggling a little closer. "You could've lost your life out there."

"Eh, I could've, but I wouldn't have," he said, adjusting his arms to wrap both around me. He kissed my forehead and declared, "I had to get back to you. That was my motivation to stay safe."

Epilogue

"Stop gassing me," I said. I looked at him, pursed my lips, and tried not to blush.

"I'm not gassing," he said with a grin. "I had to get back and make sure you didn't burn the house down."

I gawked and gave him a playful shove. "Shady boots! You see the house is still standing."

He threw his head back with laughter, and I pouted at how funny he thought his joke was. He brought his head back leveled and then attempted to pull my lips into his. "I'm just playing with you," he said.

I turned my head just in time for his lips to miss and graze my cheek before turning back and giving him a playful side-eye. He made another attempt to kiss me just as the doorbell chimed. We looked at each other with confusion, as we hadn't even reached a point of agreement on what to eat for there to be a delivery. Denzel padded to the front door as another chime rang through the house, and when he opened the door, a familiar voice made me turn in the direction of the door.

"What the hell are you doing here, Deac?" Denzel asks, making way for a version of Deacon I've never seen. The few times I've seen Deacon, he was all smiles and boisterous. Tonight, he was downcasted with reddened eyes. When Deacon slinked through the kitchen and into the living room, I noticed he had a stuffed gym bag in his hand. He dropped it at his feet and looked between Denzel and me.

"My Nessa kicked me out. Can I crash for the night?"

About the Author

Danielle Brooks (born Ashley Robinson) hails from Richmond, Virginia, with a long love for writing and reading since her school-age years. Her earliest memory of writing her first "book" was as a 5th grader in a simple five-subject notebook. She later found love in poetry, only sharing it with a few friends and family and occasionally in class. In 2023, Ashley decided to follow her pursuit to become an author, taking on her alter ego, Danielle Brooks, a name that pays homage to her identity and her family lineage. She currently still lives in Richmond with her two children, a host of family, and dear friends.

You can connect with me on:
- http://beacons.ai/daniellebrookswrites
- http://www.facebook.com/daniellebrookswrites

Subscribe to my newsletter:

✉ http://beacons.ai/daniellebrookswrites

Also by Danielle Brooks

Kenderella: Once Upon A Politician

Once upon a time, Kennedy Ellis had a chance collision with the handsome bachelor Mayor Jameson Belafonte on Valentine's Day. The night was magical, and sparks were lit, but at the end of the night, it seemed that was it. However, Mayor Belafonte's team was on a mission to clean up his reputation as a playboy to make him more in favor of the public for his pursuit of Governor of Greenbrook, and he set his eyes on Kennedy as his fake girlfriend. Will this love story stay faux or turn into a serendipitous fairytale?

Printed in Great Britain
by Amazon